Fortune

Annabel Joseph

An Ellora's Cave Publication

www.ellorascave.com

Fortune

ISBN 9781419968655
ALL RIGHTS RESERVED.
Fortune Copyright © 2010 Annabel Joseph
Edited by Jillian Bell.
Cover Design by Valerie Tibbs.

Electronic book publication October 2010
Trade paperback publication 2013

With the exception of quotes used in reviews, this book may not be reproduced or used in whole or in part by any means existing without written permission from the publisher, Ellora's Cave Publishing, Inc.® 1056 Home Avenue, Akron OH 44310-3502.

Warning: The unauthorized reproduction or distribution of this copyrighted work is illegal. Criminal copyright infringement, including infringement without monetary gain, is investigated by the FBI and is punishable by up to 5 years in federal prison and a fine of $250,000. (http://www.fbi.gov/ipr/)

This book is a work of fiction and any resemblance to persons, living or dead, or places, events or locales is purely coincidental. The characters are productions of the author's imagination and used fictitiously.

The publisher and author(s) acknowledge the trademark status and trademark ownership of all trademarks, service marks and word marks mentioned in this book.

The publisher does not have any control over and does not assume any responsibility for author or third-party Web sites or their content.

Acknowledgements
ಐ

I must first offer a million thanks and a million cranes' worth of good wishes to my friends Audrey and Rob, for inspiring this book. There is no other gift like that of inspiration.

Many thanks also to Douglas Kent of www.completeshibari.com for helping with the *shibari* aspects of this book. In writing Ryan and Kat's tale, I intentionally focused more on the sensory and emotional aspects of erotic rope play, rather than attempting to create a manual for tying the knots. To learn more about the nitty-gritty of shibari, as well as shibari safety, I highly recommend Douglas' volumes *Land* and *Air*.

Thanks also to Openflower, Fiz, Nemith, CyberKat, Malcolm and Isobel, ErickCique, Grond, Anastacia42, MasterGoliath, FrenchChris, Seer and all the other rope enthusiasts who chimed in when I put out the call for information.

Spasiba to Sascha for acting as my Russian consultant with so much patience and sweetness. And much love to my late Russian grandfather, who called me princess through all those years I needed it most.

Chapter One

Kat leaned against the wall of the tiny bathroom, feeling the pounding house music vibrate against her shoulder blades. The beat was infectious. She tapped her foot along with the rhythm, although it might have been impatience that had her toes tapping. Or the pressure in her bladder.

She had been waiting at least ten minutes and the line behind her trailed out the door. She couldn't imagine how a club as big as Masquerade got away with having two measly bathroom stalls in the ladies' room. There had to be some kind of building statute about it. Well, there were actually three stalls but at least one was always out of order. Every so often two were out of order and then the line was truly hell.

Marla, the attendant, smiled at Kat in sympathy before turning to spritz some perfume on another clubgoer. Marla was a big lady with a big heart and a big counter full of provisions. Hairspray, perfume, lotions, tampons, candy, condoms. Marla ran a tight ship—no drugs or sex in her bathroom. She kept it clean, pleasant, well lit and well stocked. If only she were capable of installing another five or six toilets…

Finally a stall door opened and Kat ducked in. She hiked up her dress, yanked down her tights and hovered over the seat, squatting rather than sitting. She wouldn't have sat on a Masquerade toilet seat for a thousand bucks. She imagined they were Petri dishes for at least thirty-five previously undiscovered sexually-transmitted diseases. *Blech.*

Ah, so much better. Tights up, dress down again. She checked to be sure no sodden toilet paper was stuck to the bottom of her black patent platform shoes. They were her favorite pair, even scuffed up and worn down as they were. She had a habit of attaching sentimental value to anything she owned that hadn't been involved somehow in some clusterfuck. She would wear these until they died or until something whack happened while she was wearing them. And the latter would probably happen first.

She banged out of the stall to allow another straining, cross-legged girl to rush in after her. She smiled at Marla as she washed her hands. Then Marla's eyes widened.

"Oh, I got you something. Wait." The attendant dug in the tote bag beside her stool and whipped out a massive gum-filled lollipop. "I got this just for you." She winked at Kat.

Ha, very funny. Kat often helped herself to the normal-sized lollipops in Marla's candy basket, but this one was extra-extra-large. Silly large. Kat gave her a huge tip and some true laughter. It really touched her that Marla had thought to bring it for her. It was the nicest thing anyone had done for her in weeks. Sad that one of her dearest friends was the ladies' room attendant at Masquerade.

Kat unwrapped the bulbous gum-filled pop and stuck it in her mouth. It was so ridiculously huge it barely fit. She made some of the waiting girls giggle by pretending to fellate it. "Ooh baby, you're so big!"

Marla laughed and shook her head as Kat pulled some bangs into place and then sighed, blowing them right back out of place again. Lipstick, okay. Face, a little sweaty, but glowy, not gross. Eye makeup okay, no raccoon shadows, hair... Well, impossible to fix.

"Don't scowl so hard at yourself, Kat," Marla said. "Didn't your mama teach you your face would freeze like that?"

No, my mama never taught me that. She taught me a lot of things, but not that.

Kat's mother disapproved of her current life choices. *Katyusha*, she would scold, *get yourself a man. You're not getting any younger.* Kat sighed and looked at her face, her features too ethnic and strange, her eyes a weird green color, her dark curls as always a total mess. No wonder her mother just shook her head at her. *You will be the last one to find love.*

And she *knew*, Kat's mother. If anyone knew, she did. Kat's mother was a fortune-teller, a respected one—as much as anyone claiming to be a fortune-teller can be respected. She didn't have a fancy mystical name, a crystal ball or flowing, iridescent robes, but she amazed people with her insights and had a huge clientele. She amazed and disturbed Kat all the time. She didn't keep a darkened office with New Age music in which to receive her many important and wealthy clients, only a crowded, noisy, estrogen-filled Victorian on the west side of Boston.

Kat had three older sisters and two younger. All of them had husbands and most had children. At twenty-eight, with no man and no children, Kat was the aberration of the family. *You are the smartest one,* her mother mourned. *Why are you still alone?*

You tell me, Mama. I don't know. Tell me what my future holds. More and more it seemed to her that life was hopelessly random. She figured the whole fortune-telling thing was a crock of bullshit. Sure, sometimes her mom hit on some pretty amazing truths, but it had to be luck or simple percentages. Any guess would be right around fifty percent of the time. No, Kat didn't believe it, not for a second. Life was random. There was no way to know what was coming and no sure way to get where you wanted to go.

Her father at least understood her. He was aloof, secretive and silent like her. *Elena, let her be. She is a perfect, beautiful princess just as she is.* Her father remained eternally convinced she was a princess, although she'd long since been sullied by non-princes of every pedigree. He called her Princess more than he called her Katya or Katyusha, or even Ekaterina, her real name.

Her father had been a spy for many years, a bona fide Russian spy for the State Department. He had returned home a bit strange, although they loved him just the same. He had been very good at his work—too good. So good that he seemed to have lost some memory of who he was. Sometimes when speaking to him, it wasn't clear if he was answering as himself or someone else he was in his mind. In that way they were alike, because Kat wasn't sure who she was either. It seemed patently unfair that she, the daughter of a fortune-teller and a spy, was not more savvy and all-knowing, that she didn't have the world at her feet. But no. She didn't know anything and didn't understand anything, including herself. She was just a listless, lonely club girl with few friends and a dead-end job translating textbooks into Russian.

But all that—her job, her crazy parents and sisters and nephews and nieces and loud crowded home in West Boston—that was her other life. This was her real life. The clubs. She kept the two lives separate as much as she could. The club was her crystal ball, the only future she cared about, at least for the moment. The darkness, the swirling mist of fake smog and cigarette smoke. The press of bodies, the familiar faces every week—the only fortune she wanted to know. The music drowning out the emptiness, and later, if she wished it, strong arms around her, making her feel good until they slept and she could steal away. In this life she was not Ekaterina or Katyusha or Katya. She was just Kat, simple and easy to understand. Just a simple girl who wanted to become nothing, rub up against nothing, who didn't want to face all the questions of what life was about.

She checked her teeth for lipstick, wrangled her bangs one last time, then left Marla and made her way back out to the club. The bathrooms opened right onto the dance floor so if you just kept walking you'd be swept into the fray. She pushed her way through the writhing bodies, passing by at least three guys she remembered fucking. They ignored her just as she ignored them. A quick glance at the bouncer near the bar, then up the stairs and in and out among people until she'd threaded her way up to the balcony.

The balcony was her spot. It was crowded, but not as crowded as downstairs, so you could actually get some air. Her favorite spot was near the DJ booth. She loved to watch him sort through his CDs and cue them up, his face screwed into a mask of concentration. She slept with every DJ she could get her hands on. She'd slept with this one too. Sam or Glenn or something. He'd been very nice. He was still very nice to her, always asking what she wanted him to play.

But she didn't sleep with the bouncers, not ever. That was a rule she stuck to judiciously, even though it was hard sometimes. DJs, yes. Bartenders, sometimes. The band, of course—but bouncers, no. Bouncers were, for her anyway, too protective and noble to debase with empty sex.

The best nights were nights when someone punchy was in the bar, when fights started up and the bouncers descended on them, flew down off their perches and broke up the fights with a hardened intensity that was spellbinding to watch. They picked up guys, no matter what size they were, dangled them from headlocks and carried them like refuse out to the curb. *No fighting. You might hurt the women. We protect women around here.*

Actually, they were protecting the club from a lawsuit, but she let her mind wander where it would. She loved to imagine when they scanned the dance floor, the bar, the bathrooms, that they were carefully scanning for women in distress. Every so often a woman *would* be in distress, harassed by some guy or involved in a catfight with another woman, so they too would be carried out, although not in a headlock.

But the most gripping occurrence, for Kat anyway, was when a woman passed out. They would sweep the hapless female up in their arms, romantic-hero style, to protect her from harm. Actually, all they did was carry the hapless female outside and set her on the curb until she came to and they could call a cab for her. But Kat didn't think about that part, only the part where they lifted the woman's limp and helpless form into their strong arms.

Lucky, lucky girls who drank to inebriation. How Kat wished, just once, to be one of those girls. To give everything up and slump to the floor, to be rescued and cradled in the arms of a man. A man like the bouncers, stern and impassive and solid. Unfortunately she was way too afraid to be that passed-out girl, even though she would have loved, just once, to experience it.

But she could fantasize about it and she did from her place upstairs where she could see every bouncer in the club. The ones by the dance floor were the burliest and wore the most intimidating scowls. Kat knew all this because she came to Masquerade every Friday and Saturday night. Sundays she went to the gay club, Mondays to the Irish bar when she was up for it. Tuesdays she went to the dark, trembling emo club. Wednesdays she took off, Thursdays she went to a jazz bar sometimes and then it was Friday again and here she was.

The fact that she reviled this glitzy hipster club and everyone who patronized it didn't stop her from returning. Why? Because nobody knew her here and everyone left her alone. She could approach any of these shallow, sweaty college students or tourists or yuppies without any fear of rejection. Ninety-nine times out of one hundred she got exactly what she wanted, which was shallow, sweaty hook-up sex. Thank goodness for Marla and her unending supply of rubbers.

Kat swept her gaze from her favorite bouncers to the mass of humanity on the dance floor. She watched for a prospective boy toy to materialize. It was busy tonight, wall-to-wall. Some pretty women as always, but many more guys. She spotted one who looked promising—tall, built, with an earnest expression. She wondered why the other women weren't all over him. Maybe he had some awful flaw, like bad breath, a lisp or a mousy demeanor. With his body, Kat didn't care, so she kept watching. She'd give it awhile longer, then make her move.

Fortune

Kat looked back at the bouncer by the stairs and found him looking at her. Not just looking at her. He and his friend were talking about her. The bouncer looked away, caught, but the friend kept on staring. She didn't like the way he stared, as if he were judging her. Kat pulled the lollipop out of her mouth and made some suggestive licking motions before plunging it back between her lips. If he was going to stare, she would give him a show for shits and giggles. She could still feel him watching even though she'd looked away.

Kat had seen the guy here many times actually, hanging out with the bouncers. He always looked at her in that same reproachful way. She supposed he knew what she got up to every week, not that it was any of his business. Since she didn't sleep with bouncers or their bouncer-wannabe friends, she didn't really care if he thought her slutty or undesirable. He was nice to look at though. Tall, bronze, dark-haired like her. He was muscular, not in a beefy-bouncer way, but in the way of a guy you knew would prevail in a fight just because he was so alpha. She looked back to find him still staring. *I know why you're here. I don't approve of it.* Somehow Kat knew he was the one in one hundred who would turn her down if she propositioned him.

She looked away, lifting her chin, sucking on her lollipop. *Stare all you want, fucker. I don't give a fuck.* Stupid eye-contact games. She could play them too. *Whatever.* She came here to have fun, not get all bent out of shape over the one guy in the bar who put her off her game.

But she still watched him out of the corner of her eye, so she knew the moment he headed toward her. He took the stairs two at a time. Broad shoulders, long thigh muscles flexing as he ascended. She looked away, pretending total disinterest. He was probably coming upstairs to see someone else. A moment passed and then she felt a touch, featherlight, on the small of her back. Just light fleeting contact, but she almost shivered. He leaned next to her on the banister, not close like he was hitting on her, nor too far away. He leaned over a perfect distance from her and pinned her with dark brown eyes.

"Candy will rot your teeth, you know."

His smile was breathtaking. He was all tan healthiness, white, straight teeth and sensual lips. She slowly pulled the lollipop out of her mouth, determined not to react to his hotness or his proximity.

"I like candy. It's an addiction."

He pointed to her glass of ice water. "But you never drink."

"How do you know I don't drink?"

"Because I see you here every week and you never drink anything but water."

"You're monitoring my vices?"

"Should I be?"

He raised his eyebrows. She didn't know whether to laugh or run away. He was flirting with her and as much as she liked it, she had a panicked sense of the tables being turned. He was in control right now, not her. She sucked the cherry-red lollipop back into her mouth and chose not to reply, trying to gain the upper hand.

"What's your name?" he asked. "Why do you come here so much?"

"What's your name, and why do *you* come here so much?"

"I asked first."

She stared into his eyes, saw the corners of his lips quirk. Then he totally caved.

"Okay. My name is Ryan." He held out his hand and she shook it. He was a big man. It was so much more apparent close up than when he was standing beside an equally large bouncer at the bottom of the stairs. His hand completely engulfed hers. "And I am here a lot because I do training for the bouncers now and again."

"What kind of training?"

"Martial arts. Safe takedown. Things like that." *Safe takedown.* *Why did that sound so sexy when he said it?* She pictured him rolling on a condom before he pulled her to the floor. Probably not what he meant by safe takedown. She ran her gaze up and down his body. He was fit all right. Maybe early thirties. God, his eyes... They were killing her. They were such a rich, deep brown, fringed by dark lashes, but that wasn't what really captivated her. It was the alert intelligence in his gaze. It was ten times more seductive than his biceps. And ten times more threatening to her. She rolled the lollipop around on her tongue, pretending polite indifference.

"So you're like, one of those karate sensei guys?"

He laughed. "No. I'm a brain surgeon, but I do karate too."

She rolled her eyes. "A brain surgeon. Right."

His crooked, easy smile unnerved her. He was so damn...healthy. So solid and nonrandom. She didn't really know how to relate to that or how to deal with the feelings he aroused in her. *No. No bouncers. Or bouncer trainers.*

"So I told you my name and why I'm here so much," he said. "Your turn."

"My name is Kat and I come here to watch people." She threw him a flirty glance and smacked suggestively on the lollipop, only to receive another one of those reproachful looks.

Whatever. She decided to head back to the dance floor. She didn't come to Masquerade to get the third degree from a fine man who didn't approve of her. Where was that fucking idiot earnest-faced pretty boy when she needed him? Stupid brain-surgeon-bullshitter with his huge warm hands and his creepy stare. She infused as much flounce as she possibly could into her "well, bye" and started down the steps before he could say anything else.

"Hey, baby." A gruff voice and clammy hand stopped her near the bottom. Arms fastened around her waist, pulling her against a pudgy torso. She pushed away, rolling her eyes at the drunk guy, but he didn't take the hint. He tightened his arms.

"Hey, gorgeous. I've been watching you all night. Come dance with me."

"No. I don't want to dance. Let go of me. I was just leaving."

"You don't have to leave here all alone."

"Believe me, I want to."

"Oh, baby, come on. Don't be like that. I can put a smile on those lips. I'll give you something really sweet to suck on."

Then he leaned in so fast that she didn't have time to stop him, otherwise she would have punched him in the face. He laid a kiss on her, stabbing his tongue between her lips. She pushed him away with all the strength she had.

"Ewww!" she said in a voice loud enough to shame him. She put the lollipop back in her mouth to take the sour alcohol taste of his kiss away. *Blech, no kissing. No.* She didn't even kiss the ones she liked. She wouldn't even have kissed tall, dark and handsome karate guy, staring down at her from the top of the stairs. *Okay?* his expression seemed to ask. *Everything okay?*

No, everything's not okay. Everything's so fucking sucky I can barely stand it.

She wiped off her lips and pushed past the kiss-stealer. She was done for the night. "Just fucking leave me alone," she yelled back over her shoulder. She didn't know if she yelled it at dark eyes or icky lips.

As she stormed off, she wondered if Ryan was watching her go.

Ryan watched her walk out the door, all tight skirt and beautiful ass. Gorgeous, shapely legs in black patent shoes.

Kat. So early for her to be gone. He'd wanted to ask her if she was okay but she'd flown without a backward glance.

Anyway, she wasn't okay, not at all. Now that he'd talked to her, he was sure of that. She was just generally *not* okay. He'd seen enough of her shenanigans to know she was confused, troubled and too beautiful for her own good. He never should have talked to her. She was more fun to watch from afar. Close up, the sadness rolled off her in waves.

He'd only worked a few months or so with the bouncers, a fun sideline from his rather stressful day job and an outlet for the martial arts training he'd practiced for years. The first time he saw her was his second week there and he'd noticed her nearly every weekend since. There was something about her that fascinated him. It was probably the fact that she was the only person in the bar who didn't seem to be having fun. He hadn't seen her smile once—not when she danced, not when she talked to the various beefcake guys she hooked up with. His gut feeling was that she needed a good hard spanking. His hand twitched to give her one. That wasn't the only thing that twitched when she was around.

But she wasn't exactly girlfriend material and he wasn't going to keep up the club gig much longer. It was easy money, but he didn't need money. He was getting too old for the club life. He had a career as a neurosurgeon to concentrate on. He was closer to forty than he cared to think about and his best friend had recently married and become dad to an adorable baby son. Ryan had bounced the little critter on his knee over the holidays and been astounded at the changes in Dave and his wife. The three of them used to play kinky sex games together. They still did, but now Sophie and Dave were coupled up, their own family unit.

Ryan discovered to his shock that he wanted that too. Very much. So getting involved with a flighty club girl probably wasn't the best move at the moment. He didn't know why he'd even talked to her. It was just that she was almost painfully attractive to him. She was so much his type that she was *the* prototype for him, everything he liked in a girl. Big boobs but not too big. Little waist, tight abs, curvy little hips. An ass that was criminally tempting. What he wouldn't give to have that ass in his hands. Her face was exotic, memorable. He had never seen her smile but even her frown was attractive, even the ambivalent absentia that usually resided on her face.

Now she had a name. Kat. Something about her actually brought a cat to mind. A kitten, a Persian, a pussy... *Okay.* But she had this feline appeal. Something about the slow, graceful way she moved and her green, almond-shaped eyes. Like a cat, she exuded an air of mystery, along with an air of *fuck you.* But at the same time, she possessed a vulnerability that made him ache for her, that made him want to care for her. Whether she intended it or not, she set off his Dom radar like an alarm. He'd played around in BDSM circles for years and dated tons of beautiful, submissive girls with smiling eyes and lovely bodies he could bury himself in. He'd learned how to handle them, how to thrill them and perhaps most importantly, how to pick them out of a crowd. He could spot a submissive girl a mile away and there were tons of them out there. Some aware, some not so aware, but all predictably compliant once they were in his hands.

But her... Well... He just didn't know.

She seemed to almost revile men, the same men she constantly left with at last call. It was clear to Ryan that none of the men she left with fulfilled her. He'd see her the following weekend avoiding them like the plague. She was a wanton, a siren—but she was angry. Angry and slutty were never a good mix. He was pretty sure she also had a nihilistic, self-destructive streak. The Dominant side of him wanted to attain her and then tame her, but another part of him knew that would be difficult if not impossible. *I want to fix you. I want your submission, your obedience, your body. You'll like it.* What would she do if he approached her that way?

He didn't want her as a one-night stand. He didn't want to be one more notch on her hook-up belt, although he was certain he could have accomplished it easily. That held no interest for him. He wanted her as his submissive or not at all. He wanted her, from the start, kneeling at his feet. Unfortunately, she seemed more apt to kick him in the nuts.

Well, no matter. There were plenty of fish in the sea and plenty of submissive women looking for a Dominant. He would be a fool to get mixed up with her, as tempting as the fantasy was. He wasn't going after her. Not now, not ever. No.

* * * * *

Kat hit the pavement and started walking. She was so wrought-up that she chose to walk the few blocks to her house, even though a cab would have been safer at this time of night. She didn't know why she was so unhinged tonight. Guys at the club accosted her all the time. She supposed it was because *he'd* watched the whole thing, he of the knowing eyes and judgmental smile. He'd seen that guy force his kiss on her, seen her push him away, seen her wipe her mouth and yell at the jerk like a child. He had talked to her like she was a child, like he knew better than her. Or maybe it was just her thinking that.

What made Kat most angry was that he didn't come save her, didn't come bounding down the stairs to her defense. Didn't level the guy with one well-placed punch to the windpipe and drag his sorry ass outside. And now there was no earnest-faced boy to go home with, only her own empty bed in her family's house near Brighton.

When she got home, she climbed the stairs to the porch heavily. She could hear a crying baby even from outside. Her sister Olga's one-month-old. Darling during the day, devil all night. Kat brushed past her, suddenly bone-tired.

"Kat, rock the baby for me, please," Olga begged. "Just for an hour. You're always up at night."

She didn't even stop. "He's not my baby. I'm tired. I smell like smoke."

"I'm tired too. I've been up for hours. Please. *Pozhaluĭsta*, Katya."

"No," Kat said again, hating herself. She tumbled into bed, pulling the pillow over her head so she didn't have to hear the baby wailing. It didn't help.

She lay awake a long time thinking about Mr. Dark Eyes, thinking about the way he would have looked at her for not helping her sister. He knew she was a bad, selfish person. He knew.

Fortune

Chapter Two
⚜

She came back again the following night, of course. Clockwork. Ryan wanted to talk to her again now that he'd made her acquaintance, even if it was just another awkward, defensive exchange. *No. Too difficult. Not worth it.* He finally convinced himself to leave her alone but he couldn't stop watching her. Why did she fascinate him so much?

She danced for a while when it got busier, when the bodies were pressed together on the dance floor. He watched her from behind the bar, which wasn't difficult because she jumped up on the platform below the DJ booth. It was like the music possessed her, like the beats lived inside her. He liked house music as much as the next clubgoer, but she seemed to really know the music, feel it deeply. Her hips moved, her feet stomped, her hands reached up in the air and then everyone was jumping, riled up by the beat. For some, it was joy and release. But for her, it seemed an opportunity to lose herself. He felt his cock rising in response to her sexy movements, her curvy body and lovely legs.

By the time she retired to her favored spot up on the balcony, he knew—against his better judgment—that he was going to go talk to her again. *One last chat*, he told himself. *This is the absolute last time you talk to this girl.* She ignored him as he approached and leaned beside her on the rail.

"Hi there, Kat. Back again, I see."

A corner of her lip turned down. "Just like you."

God, the pull was excruciating. Her little black dress fit her so well it was criminal.

"My name's Ryan, in case you don't remember."

She shot him a look. "I remember. I just don't feel like talking, Ryan. No offense."

"I'm not offended. But why don't you feel like talking?"

"The music is too loud. It's too hard to hear."

He leaned closer and spoke next to her ear. "Can you hear me better now?"

She drew away and looked at him. For the first time Ryan saw a spark of the real girl, not the mannequin, before her face rearranged itself into apathy. "What do you want from me?"

"I want to know why you never smile."

She looked away again. "I smile when I feel like it."

The timeless dance of flirtation and rebuttal. She looked like she would gladly toss him over the balcony if she could.

"You know what, Kat? I think you're a very pretty girl."

She snorted. "That's the greatest line I've ever heard. Seriously. Only a brain surgeon could come up with something so original."

"You don't believe I'm really a brain surgeon?"

"Let me put it this way. I wouldn't have a lot of respect for a brain surgeon who hung out in a crap club like this every weekend."

"You hang out here."

"Don't remind me."

He could have pulled out his medical ID and showed it to her, but he was so used to girls going all weak at the knees because of his career that he kind of enjoyed the novelty of her disregard.

"So I guess the next question is obvious," he said. "Why do you hang out here if you hate it so much?"

She crossed her arms over her chest. "I would love to answer that question for you but I don't really know."

"Which points at a rather alarming level of non-self-awareness."

"Non-self-awareness? Is that even a word?"

"I know a lot of large and exotic words, being a brain surgeon."

She rolled her eyes. "I think I'm going to go dance."

He laughed as she pushed away from the railing and made her way through groups of people to the stairs. She was a little sassafras, that was for sure. He watched her squeeze between two gabbing club girls and extricate herself from a groping drunk guy. He was just thinking how disappointed he was that he wasn't going to talk to her again when he saw her fall off balance. She teetered just a moment and then tumbled down the stairs.

It was like slow motion. He saw every contact with the hard concrete, calculating possible bodily damage. *Ouch, her shoulder...her hip.* She almost righted herself, but then flipped around and fell backward hard, her head hitting the metal edge of the last stair. He was already halfway down behind her, pushing people out of the way.

As he bent over her, she looked up at him, pained and confused. Behind her head, he could already see the blood. Head injuries bled copiously, he knew, so he tried not to panic. He attempted to check her limbs without moving her, wary of spinal damage, but she struggled to sit up.

"Just lie still," he said. "Don't try to move yet." He pushed her back down as forcefully as he dared. Kevin, one of the bouncers, looked over his shoulder.

"She's bleeding all over the place."

"Yeah, that happens when people crack their heads open. Can't you move these gawkers away from here?" Ryan asked, gesturing around.

The bouncers began cordoning off the stairs like some kind of crime scene. One of them handed him a pair of gloves. Ryan pressed his hand hard against the wound on the back of her scalp.

"Ouch," she moaned.

"Just be still. What hurts?"

"Everything." But she moved her arms and legs enough to reassure him her spine was okay. He scowled up at the ocean of drunk partygoers around them, noticing guys leering at her. *Bloody chick, cool.* Idiots. He pushed down her skirt so they couldn't look up her dress. Stupid, worrying about them gawking at her panties at a time like this. He leaned over her, pressing on the gash, worrying about brain injuries and skull fractures.

"Let me up," she muttered, pushing at his hands.

"I would prefer not to until I know the bleeding has stopped."

"I'm still bleeding?"

"Like a fountain. Now be still until the ambulance gets here."

"Who called an ambulance? I can't afford an ambulance."

"The club will cover it. Head and neck injuries are nothing to take chances with. Now hush and lie still."

"You know I... I really don't do well with blood...and needles..."

"You're going to need stitches for a start. And if there's any cranial bleeding—"

She made a sound halfway between a protest and a plea and promptly passed out.

* * * * *

The first thing Kat saw when she came awake was the jumbled collection of origami figures on the tray beside her. At first she thought it was crumpled scraps of newspaper. Her eyes focused, her mind still fuzzy. *Not scraps. Origami. That's strange.* She turned with a start to find a familiar set of dark eyes looking at her, then back down at her chart. The man from Masquerade was standing at the foot of her bed in a white lab coat. *Shit.*

"So you really are a doctor."

"I don't lie, Ekaterina. Ever. Yes, I am a doctor. A surgeon, actually, but let's not quibble over terms."

Ekaterina. He knew her full name now, and god knew what else and he was looking down at her in full asshole-doctor mode. What the hell was his name again? Brian? Ryan? She gestured to her chart. "Why are you looking at that? That's my private information."

"I'm the neuro specialist on call this morning, so for the moment you're my patient. Dr. Ryan McCarthy," he said, flashing his badge at her before sitting down on the edge of the bed. Kat was mortified to think how awful she probably looked. It was impossible to meet his eyes now, with his scrubs and the lanyard of medical IDs around his neck and that curt, bedside-manner way he spoke to her. "How are you feeling?" he asked. He reached out and she thought he meant to hold her hand but he took her wrist instead and pressed his forefinger to her pulse.

"What time is it?" she asked.

"Six in the morning. I just came on shift."

"But you were here last night with me."

"Yes."

"When do you sleep?"

"How are you feeling?" he repeated with an edge of impatience.

"Horrible." The back of her head ached like hellfire. She reached up behind her, remembering her fall and the bleeding.

"Don't touch." His voice arrested her. "You're bandaged up pretty good."

"Am I bald in the back now?"

He laughed with that easy, white-toothed smile she remembered. "They don't normally shave patients bald just to put in a few stitches. Most of your hair is still there."

She vaguely remembered that now, the stitches, the scans of her brain. IVs and ambulance lights and people shining flashlights in her eyes. He made some notes in her chart. "What are you writing?" she asked suspiciously.

"That you're making conversation and seem relatively alert this morning."

"Oh."

"How does your head feel? Sore, achy? Any sharp pain?"

"Just...sore. Woozy."

"They sedated you last night. You really don't do well with medical procedures."

She grimaced. "I never have."

"No big deal. At least you slept well. How's your vision?"

She shrugged, watching the way his fingers toyed with the pen in his hand, flipping it around in a circle. Dark tufts of hair on tan knuckles. Big, big fingers. *Jesus, Kat. Just chill.* "My vision is fine. So will I live?"

"I sincerely hope so. At least try not to die on my shift. They frown on that."

He pulled a small penlight out of his pocket and turned it on, then took her chin between those big fingers and leaned close, shining it into her eyes. She stared forward, trying not to think about the subtle pressure of his thumb and forefinger, or how near he was to her. Or how shivery both those things made her feel. Good lord, she'd bled all over him last night, whined about the procedures and needles. She'd probably even cried at some point. It's not like he would feel any attraction to her now, whether he'd flirted with her at Masquerade or not. Had that been just last night that he'd smiled and flirted with her? Just last night that she'd gone pitching down the stairs like a total idiot? It seemed a world away now.

He pulled back, made more notes, all businesslike doctor. Some part of her wanted him to smile that big smile at her again, to acknowledge her as more than his patient, but he was all serious and professional.

"Your brain scans and x-rays look good. They'll do another set this afternoon and then tomorrow morning, and provided they look the same, they'll probably let you go home. Your mother will be happy to hear it. She was a little upset last night."

Kat caught her breath. "A little upset?"

"They almost had to call security."

As if on cue, her mama swept into the room, waving her arms around in wide, dramatic gestures and yelling at the top of her lungs. Four of Kat's sisters pushed into the room too and Ryan stepped back from the bed as they crowded around Kat.

"Katyusha! You crazy girl!" her mother shrieked, then turned and glared at Ryan. He was a pretty big man and pretty well built, but he backed away from her. Most men did. "You are still here?"

"I actually work here, Mrs. Argounov."

Her mother's gaze fell on the pile of origami figures before fixing back on the man in the white coat.

"What is your name, you? Your name is?"

"Ryan. Dr. Ryan McCarthy."

"Doctor? So you are her doctor now?" Her mother had a thick Russian accent, so it sounded like *duk-ter*.

"I'm a surgeon, actually."

Mama clutched her chest. "She had surgery? When did this happen? I knew I should never have left you here. My poor baby."

Kat suffered her mother's smothering hug while Ryan watched with a faint grin.

"No. Well, she didn't actually have any surgeries, Mrs. Argounova. I'm just here as a consult."

"A consult? What does this mean?"

"Mama, he's helping me," Kat interjected. "Just back off with the questions. I'm fine."

Her mother glanced over at her, then back at the man across from her, studying him with an unfathomable look in her eye.

"Mama," Kat warned in a low voice. She didn't want her doing any of her weird perceptive nonsense. Not here, not now.

"Dr. Ryan McCarthy, you have my many thanks," her mama finally managed. But she still looked at him for an unnaturally long time, long past the time she should have looked away. Then she extended one plump hand. "Please, call me Elena. You and my daughter are friends?"

He and Kat looked at each other. "No. Well—" Kat said, as Ryan said, "Yes."

"And you are good *duk-ter*? You take excellent care of her?"

"I'll do my best. But I do have a surgery to prepare for now, so I'd better go."

"Yes, you must go." Her mother nodded as if it had been her own brilliant idea, although Kat could tell he was dying to get out of there. "You go and do surgeries, yes. Many blessings on your head."

Ryan took one last look at Kat and left, brushing by her sisters. She wondered if she'd ever see him again. She wasn't sure if she wanted to or not. Her mother watched him go too, then turned to Kat, hugging her close, clucking over the bandage around her head.

"My baby girl. You see, this going out, dancing, partying all night. When they call last night, I drive here expecting the worst. *Gospodi*, a call from the hospital! I didn't tell your father. It will kill him with worry."

"I'm sorry, Mama."

"When will you outgrow this nonsense? It is time to grow up now into lady. You must find a good man and settle down. What about this *duk-ter*? He is your friend?"

"He's just...some guy. I don't know. I barely know him."

"One of your, how do they say, 'man sluts' — "

"Mama, please."

"I am only saying he is handsome, *duk-ter*, probably rich man. Maybe you get to know him better, *zaika*."

"Life is not all about bagging a rich man, Mama."

"I didn't ever say rich man was all in life. I never did. Is your father a rich man? Not so much. What is important is to find a man who makes you happy. You, girl. You run around, you wear your short skirts and clonky shoes and your hair..." Elena sighed, lifting a tangled mass of Kat's curly locks from beneath the bandage.

Kat pulled away. "I got this tragic hair from you, you realize."

"Don't take that tone with me." Her mother enfolded her in another smothering hug, pressing her to her ample chest. "Katyusha, my own. I only want you to be happy. It is my wish for you, my one wish. You know this."

"Yes, Mama. I know. But it's not that simple. I can't just pretend to be happy, or bag some rich doctor and find happily ever after."

"I know. You must find your way. You *will* find your way. I know this." She pulled away and smiled down at Kat with a twinkle in her eye. "You know I do know, *zaika*."

"Did your crystal ball tell you?"

"My heart tells me, you impossible brat. Now you rest. You get better, Katyusha mine."

* * * * *

Later, after Ryan's last surgery, he went to her floor and checked in at the nurses' station. "Ekaterina Argounov," he said, repeating the exotic name he'd learned from her chart. She had pronounced her mother's name "ma*ma*," with the accent on the second syllable. Her ethnicity fascinated him, like everything else about her.

His last surgery had run over, although it was ultimately successful. He hated to admit how antsy he'd gotten at the end, how impatient he was to see her—the girl he definitely didn't want to get messed up with. But things were feeling messier than ever right now. He fought with himself as he walked down the quiet, sterile hallway. Why was he here when he had no intention of getting tangled up with her?

He stopped outside the door, looking through the window. The ma*ma* was sitting in Kat's room by the bed. Kat was sitting up too, alert and awake. Her eyes flitted to his over her mother's shoulder, her beautiful eyes that made him forget everything. Elena turned and saw him too.

"Dr. Ryan McCarthy! You come in." Not *would you like to come in?* Not *why don't you join us?* It was an order as emphatic as any he'd received as a child. He pushed the door open slowly as Kat stared daggers at him.

"I know you're tired. I won't stay. I just came by to—"

"Come in and sit," Elena ordered, getting up. "I have to go to...gift shop. You stay here, you sit with her. You stay, yes? While I am gone?"

He was pretty sure the gift shop was closed, but he sat in the chair Elena shoved him toward and watched her sail out the door.

He studied Kat. Good, she looked better. Some part of him had feared a hidden pocket, a slow bleed. He worried all day about being paged for emergency surgery. He couldn't have done it, not on her.

"You don't have to stay," she said at the same time he asked, "How are you feeling?"

They both paused. "I'm feeling okay," Kat finally said. "Less groggy. I'm sorry about my mother, she's a little—"

"Never apologize for your mother," he said in a chiding tone that doubtlessly annoyed her. She stopped talking and stared at her hands. The awkward silence was stultifying. *Just leave, you idiot.* "So no pain? No visual disturbances?" *Okay, that's not leaving.*

"No bad pain. Just the bruises. And the twenty stitches along the back of my head," she added ruefully.

"Maybe I should just take a look while I'm here." *Idiot. Not your job! Leave now, before you touch her. If you touch her...* She leaned forward and he put one hand on her hair even though he didn't need to. He felt guilty, like one of those doctors who fondled patients on the sly. Her curls were as thick and soft as he imagined. He ran a thumb across her nape as he lifted the gauze to check the stitches. When she shivered a little he almost came undone. He replaced the bandage quickly and stepped back.

"They look good, Kat. And any scar won't show unless you pull your hair up. I'd say you're a very lucky lady to come away with just a scar, considering the fall you took. But you'll need to take things easy for a while. No late nights and bar hopping. No tabletop dancing."

She looked at him with that shuttered, slanted glance, and again he thought, *Go, just go. Get out of here.* This wasn't the wanton tease from the club. This was a real girl and he felt even more strongly for her. Forget messing with her stitches, the medical small talk. He wanted to take her in his arms. Why this strange pull, this connection? Yesterday it had been all about the amazing body, the challenge of the frown. Now, he realized, it was about something more. She looked back down at her hands, a faint blush rising in her pale cheeks.

"I do appreciate your help. For you to stay all night... And I know I bled all over you."

He shrugged and smiled. "You really know how to maim yourself. But you're okay, and that's all that matters."

"Well... Thank you. I wouldn't have liked to bleed out at the bottom of the stairs at Masquerade."

"No. It wouldn't have been a very dignified way to go."

She looked up at him, her deep green eyes narrowed in a question. "You seem awfully young to be a surgeon."

"Thank you. But I'm not that young."

"You're younger than every other surgeon I've ever seen."

"And how many have you seen?"

She pursed her lips and he grinned by way of apology. "Okay, you're right. I'm slightly younger than average. I started college early."

"When you were twelve?"

"Not quite," he hedged. He had been almost sixteen.

"You're like Doogie Howser, huh? Child genius?"

"I was just really motivated. I always wanted to be a surgeon. My parents were both surgeons."

"They were? They died?"

"They retired last year. Went off to spend their golden years in Aruba."

"Oh, nice."

Her *Oh, nice* was difficult to decipher. Approval? Derision? He mentally compared his serious, reserved parents with the effusive Elena Argounov. He loved his parents, but his childhood had been lonely, quiet. Solitary. He wondered what Kat's childhood had been like, with her prodigious mother and all those women he'd assumed were sisters since they all looked like different versions of Kat.

"Did you make these?" Kat asked, turning to the window. Someone, perhaps her mother, had lined up all his little origami figures like soldiers on the windowsill beside her bed. He'd made a cat, a dog, a crane, a fish, a pig, a tiger and even a bird with flappable wings. Kid stuff. He could fold more complicated things, but that took a level of concentration he hadn't possessed last night as he watched her sleep and obsessed about intracerebral hemorrhage and aggravated axonotmesis.

"Yeah. I've been making those for ages. I make them for kids sometimes before surgeries to calm their nerves."

"You're like Patch Adams."

"Patch Adams. Doogie Howser. Any other celebrity doctors you'd like to compare me to?"

She laughed then, a weak laugh, but it was a laugh. He stared at the way her face changed when she smiled. It was over too soon.

"Do that again."

"Do what?"

"Laugh. Or at least smile. I thought you weren't capable of it."

She snorted softly, with another quick smile that left him wanting more.

"I wonder what it would be like to see you laugh until you were breathless." His words came without thought, without intention. She sobered and looked down at her hands, then back at him. They were still looking at each other when Elena returned.

"*Ouft*," she sighed. "Gift shop is closed. But thank you for staying. You think she is okay? She go home soon?"

"Tomorrow, I expect," Ryan said. "Her physician will be by to discharge her."

Elena dug in her purse, brought out a business card and handed it to him.

"You come to our house so Ekaterina's papa can give thanks to you. She is his princess. He will wish to thank you very much. He is not so strong in his mind now and he does not like hospitals, so he cannot come here," she said. "You come and see us. Come for dinner."

He looked down at the card. *ELENA ARGOUNOV, FORTUNE-TELLER AND SPIRITUAL ADVISOR*. And under that, in ornate, swirly script, "Show me your palm and I will tell you your future."

"You call first if you like, let us know you are coming. A big boy like you, an important doctor has great appetite, yes? I cook lots of food."

The phone number was there, the address too. Unbearable temptation.

"Thanks, Mrs. Argounov, but I have consultations, office hours. Surgeries of course, and then work at the club some evenings—"

"You call and you come," Kat's mother snapped in her inimitable style.

"Yes, I sure will," he assured her. "When things slow down, I'll call."

But he wouldn't call. He absolutely *would not* call. Kat watched him pocket the card, watched the entire interaction with an ambivalent look on her face. Oh, her glorious curls and those lovely pouting lips he wanted to kiss.

Run, you idiot. Run.

Forget it. It's too late.

Chapter Three
ಸಿ

It took over a week for Kat to get back on her feet. Then she started work from home, which was impossible with all the noise, so she returned to working at the office probably sooner than she should have. Her stitches itched and her bruises were tender. She went straight to bed after work, no nightclubs. Her beloved club shoes were tainted by misfortune and went out with the trash.

She still thought about him, though, in no small part because her mother muttered often about the fact that he didn't call. Kat tried not to care, but each time she stood at the top of a flight of stairs, she felt the loss of him. She waited for it to happen again, some random accident in the random world that flummoxed her. Wouldn't he be sorry when her next stair debacle turned fatal because he wasn't there? Escalators with their sharp, scary teeth were impossible for her to cope with. She took elevators whenever she could and convinced herself he was just an asshole. Just one more of those club guys, not worth obsessing over. She forced herself to stop thinking about him and actually tried to convince herself she hated him. She threw away his silly paper animals so she didn't have to look at them, then fished them out of the trash and stowed them in a shoebox under the bed because she couldn't bear to lose them.

On difficult days, when the textbook translation was boring and her family was annoying her to tears, she'd pull out the box and pore over the origami figures he'd made. The folds and corners were so delicate and precise. Little flaps and notches, each perfectly symmetrical and balanced, like him. She would trace the folds as if to trace the fingers that had run over them. Some of the newspaper ink blurred along the edges. Had his fingers done that? Or hers, tracing again and again? She imbued the paper figurines with an emotional gravity she was sure they didn't have.

She just needed to go back out to the clubs. She needed the eardrum-bursting music, the hot press of party people. But to return to that place where she'd surely see him, where she'd have to navigate those stairs—it seemed the most self-destructive of choices.

But then, she was a self-destructive person. It took less than three weeks for her to break down and return to Masquerade because she simply couldn't stay away. She refused to admit to herself that he was the reason, that she really wanted to see *him* again. She convinced herself it was only the atmosphere she missed, and the promise of more empty but comforting sex.

When she got there it felt strangely different. She felt like an outsider for the first time in a long time. She wandered around for a while, then retreated to her place at the top of the stairs, navigating the concrete steps gingerly. The blood was long gone, of course, and now the stairs had some kind of nonslip rubber material on them. Some other girls were standing in her spot. *Damn it.* She leaned on the railing farther down and her gaze swept the dance floor. Lots of new faces but a few familiar ones too.

But not him. *Relax*, she told herself. *You didn't come here to see him.* She could have asked one of the bouncers where Ryan was but she was way too embarrassed to do that. Even now, she thought they were looking at her funny. *Why is she back here? I hope she doesn't fall down the stairs again.* She needed to get out of there before she went crazy, but she needed to find a man first.

She made her way down to the dance floor and found a hot prospect quickly, a youngish, very handsome college boy. *Okay, you'll do*, she thought to herself, pasting on a come-hither smile. He was sweaty but he still smelled good and he had some pretty intriguing hip-thrusting action going on. He leered back at her and started grinding his hips against her. He was already half-hard. Oh yes, he was hers.

But then she felt a hand close on her elbow. She pulled away instinctively. She hated to be grabbed at. Hard, dark eyes bore into hers and he wouldn't let her pull away. In fact, he was pulling her right off the dance floor.

"Let go of me." She tried to extricate herself. "How dare you? I was dancing with that guy."

"I saw your little hook-up-in-progress," Ryan muttered. He spun her to face him on the edge of the dance floor. "What in holy fuck's name are you doing back here again?"

"I'm dancing and trying to have fun. At least I was."

"You go home *now* and you go home *alone*. I'm tired of watching you do this."

"Do what?"

"Give it away and play fast and loose with your life. You're supposed to be resting, recuperating. Hm, now how would I know that? Oh, that's right. Because I was your doctor!"

"That doesn't mean you can yank me around now and tell me what to do. Why the fuck do you care anyway?"

He leaned close to her, his eyes flashing. "Because you're a reckless little slut and I do not approve."

His face was so close to hers that they could have kissed if they wanted to, but they didn't kiss. He started to pull her again. She was so shocked by his words she didn't resist when he tugged her along. The crowds parted to let them pass and she felt embarrassed that everyone was witnessing something so private. She was embarrassed by the possessive way he dragged her, by the angry look on his face. But at the same time, she was also a little aroused at the way he was manhandling her.

She caught a glimpse of College Boy, who gestured in confusion.

"No," Ryan spat at him. "Not yours."

Not yours. Whose was she? From the way he was acting, he thought she was his. He hustled her back through the kitchen and into a small storage room in the back. He turned on the light and shut and locked the door behind them.

He let go of her finally and she scrambled away. He stood between her and the door, arms crossed over his chest, legs braced apart. He looked every bit like he was about to beat her up. She was definitely scared at that moment, but not really scared that he would hurt her. No, she was that kind of scared when you just don't know what's going to happen, when the world's all weird and upside down and you suddenly realize you're standing on the edge of a cliff.

"Okay," she said, pressing back against the wall. "What do you want?"

"I want to know why you do it. These things you do."

She feigned innocence. "What things?"

"You know what things. Coming to a club you don't like, sleeping with men you don't like. It doesn't make you happy."

"How do you know?"

"Because you never smile."

She drew in a breath and frowned at him. "I don't like to smile."

"You don't like anything."

"Yes, I do."

"Name one thing you like."

"I like to be left alone," she muttered, crossing her arms over her chest to mirror him.

"Those days are over, Kat. I'm telling you that now. If you're going to come here to this club, I'm not going to stand around and let you act like a whore."

"I can do what I want and you can't fucking stop me."

"I'll say it one more time, slowly, so you'll understand." He repeated himself, each word firmly enunciated. "If you're going to come here to this club, I'm not going to stand around and let you act like a whore."

Holy fucking Christ. He really believed he had some say in the matter. She blew out her breath and stamped one foot in her new Mary Janes.

"Fine. I just won't come here then." She brushed by him to get to the door. "I'll leave right now and I won't come back. Believe me, I won't." His hand took hers and squeezed it, preventing her from unlocking the deadbolt.

"But you'll go to another place and do the same thing."

"Yes. Maybe I will."

When she tried to wrench her hand away, he gripped it tighter and moved closer to her, his body trapping hers against the door. She went still and hunched forward as if she could sink right through the solid wood and escape. But she didn't want to escape, not really. He stood behind her and she felt his solid chest rise and fall against her back, felt his breath against her ear. Then his other hand came around and cupped her chin, gently turning her face back to his.

"Oh, Kat," he said. Just two words, but something about the tender way he said them took a little of the fight out of her.

"Let go of me."

"No," he said quietly. "I wish I could but I don't think I can." He leaned down and pressed his rough cheek against hers. She was hypnotized by his closeness, his warmth, his masculine smell. She drew a shuddery breath and he drew back abruptly. She spun to face him, her eyes wide, her heart pounding. His gaze raked over her.

"Turn back around, Kat. Face the door and put your hands on it."

"I...what... Why?"

"Because I'm going to spank you."

"You can't spank me," she protested. "That's...that's illegal."

"Not exactly illegal."

"You can't do this! Why do you want to s-spank me?"

"Because you need it," he answered without missing a beat. "Now be a good girl, turn around and place your hands on the door in front of you."

"But...but... What will you... How will you... I don't even know—"

"You should just trust me."

"Trust you? I barely know you."

"I think we know each other pretty well. I know that you need some discipline in your life. You're out of control and you have been for a while. You know I know what's good for you. Better than you know yourself."

"You know better? What?" She searched for words to refute him but she was distracted by his broad chest as he crossed his arms in front of her. Those muscles... "No... Well... It's not... You don't understand."

"I think I do understand."

"You don't. It's just... It's everything else." Why on earth was she trying to explain, to reason with him? Why was she still standing here? He looked so sympathetic, so understanding, she found the words pouring out. "I'm not out of control, I'm just... It's just... Life is so random—"

"Life's not random at all. Everything happens for a reason."

"I don't believe that."

"I do."

She swallowed hard. He was so convinced. He put his hand on his belt buckle, drawing her gaze down his body to his defined waist, his thighs...and... *Gulp.*

"Now turn around."

"I d-don't want to."

"I know," he answered in a calm tone, "but I think you should."

And she did. She couldn't explain why, even as she did it. Something about the way he spoke to her both made her want to obey and made her horny as hell. She half-turned, addled, and then he put his hands on her, turned her the rest of the way. He pressed her against the door with a little squeeze on her shoulders. If she'd wanted to, she could have flipped the lock in an instant and run away in her clunky club shoes. The fact that she didn't was a choice she made—a choice that shocked her.

"Give me your hands."

She reached them back to him from where they were, clutched in a panicked ball in front of her chest. He took them in his and placed them hard against the wall on either side of her head. He stood behind her close enough that Kat could feel his chest against her back again. His hand cupped her bottom.

"You are going to stand there, Ekaterina, and I am going to spank your ass for these crazy choices you make. I hope, next time, this will help you make better choices. It's going to hurt but you're not going to move and you're not going to take your hands from the wall. Do you understand?"

She was speechless. She might have made a strangled sound of assent. She could hear the swoosh of his belt as he pulled it from the loops of his jeans. Holy fuck, he was actually going to try to spank some sense into her. He was going to use his belt on her. Never in her life had anyone spanked her, not her mother or father or any man she'd ever known. She was shaking like a leaf. She had no idea what it would feel like or why she was even accepting it.

He made a low sibilant sound as if to say she shouldn't be so scared. He backed up then and brought his belt down on her ass. *Holy fucking shit.* She bit her tongue in distress as the sting bloomed in her cheeks.

"I can't do this," she moaned, shifting on her feet.

"Yes, you can."

He hit her again and then again, each blow a little harder than the last. It stung, it smarted, each stroke built and combined into a more and more excruciating ache, but it wasn't the pain that was undoing her. It was the unfamiliar intimacy and the way her legs were growing weak with lust. She felt him behind her like a force, a pillar. She wanted him, wanted him more desperately than she'd ever wanted anyone in her life.

"Please, Ryan," she sighed. She didn't know if she was pleading with him to stop or hit her harder or take down her panties and fuck her against the wall. Another blow, and then another. She went up on her toes, her hands in fists. The hot aching sting of his belt spread like fire to her pussy. Her clit pulsed and throbbed, made her question her sanity, her perversity. *Why was this turning her on so much?* She tried to muffle her cries because they sounded obscene. There was no way he didn't know, didn't understand exactly how he was affecting her.

"Please," she begged finally, when her ass was burning and she was so hot and wet she thought she might faint. He did stop then, but only to step closer and lift up her thin silk skirt.

"No," she said, but it came out a tremulous plea, not the order she'd intended.

"Yes," he replied, hooking his fingers in the waistband of her panties and slowly drawing them down to the tops of her thighs. The rough pads of his fingers traced her flaming ass cheeks. Each stroke of his fingertips sent shivery heat along her nerves until her whole body felt electrified, possessed. What was he doing to her? How could he be so calm and matter-of-fact about it? She ground her forehead against the door, using every ounce of her strength not to reach back and cover herself, yank her panties back up and turn to him and plead…for what? She was too far gone to know and more aroused than she'd ever been in her life.

"Look at me," he said.

She shook her head. "I can't. No."

"Why not? Are you afraid? Hurt? You want me to stop?"

"Yes. No! I don't know what I want."

"Look at me," he said again, and she turned to gaze back at him, at his impassive face, his muscular arms and the brown belt doubled over and dangling from his powerful hand. If he'd wanted to turn her on, wanted her to see him so she'd want him even more, he'd found success. He raised his arm again and she watched almost until the blow fell before she turned again and screwed her eyes shut against the door.

The pain of the belt strikes had been erotic over top of her skirt and panties. On her naked ass, it was divine. She didn't know if she was supposed to be enjoying this or not so she tried to hide her arousal, but by this point he had to know. Her moans rose in intensity. She felt lost, trapped somewhere between pleasure and pain.

"Please," she said again, and now she knew she was begging and what she was begging for. He knew too. She heard him draw in his breath and stand still for a moment.

"Is that all?" she whispered.

"Just hush," he said, low and gruff and then moved forward to trap her against the door again. He was as hard as she was wet. She could feel his huge erection through his jeans. She couldn't help herself and arched back against him with a sigh. Again, he drew his breath in sharply. When he spoke his voice sounded strained. He started to undo his jeans.

"You're not going home with any boys tonight, are you?"

"No." She shook her head. "No, I won't."

"You've learned your lesson?"

"Y-yes…yes." His hand snaked down and stroked the front of her thighs, warm, gentle pressure. When he shifted and nuzzled her ear, she moaned and let him spread her legs. She leaned back against him as his fingers slid down her bare pussy and found her clit, swollen and wet. She shuddered with pleasure each time he stroked it.

"I'm glad to hear that," he whispered. "But I won't send you home like this. I'm not that mean."

"No. No. No..." It was all she could think to say, over and over. *No, you shouldn't do this. No, this is wrong. No, don't send me home, not this way.*

"No, or yes?" he asked against her ear, hot breath and rough stubble.

"Yes. Yes! Use a condom. Please."

"Of course I will. I'm glad you asked."

He already had one in his hands, yanked from some pocket or his wallet. She was still pressed to the door, skirt up, panties down, legs spread open by his knees. She felt him yanking his pants down, felt his cock spring out against her— cool, velvet steel against her flaming ass. *Oh my god.* He put on the condom, then his hands were back on her again, stroking her hip, grasping her shoulder. She didn't care anymore about discovery, about someone passing by and overhearing them. She didn't care about anything but his hands on her waist and his cock nudging her open. She moaned and he stopped.

"Okay?"

She made some desperate sound she was sure she'd never made before and shifted her hips, granting him access. With a groan he pressed forward and she let it all happen, let his hard, thick cock push up inside her all the way to the hilt, not resisting or thinking or doing anything but feeling him take her, possess her. He was so big and powerful sliding up inside her. If he hadn't been holding her she would have fallen. He withdrew and pressed in again, a slow slide and delicious ache. He took her hips in his hands and pulled her back against him so even if she'd wanted to escape she couldn't have gotten away.

She cried out so loudly at the crippling pleasure of the next thrust that he put his hand over her mouth. Not hard enough to steal her breath, just hard enough to muffle the sounds she couldn't control anymore. She couldn't control anything. Oh god. *Oh god.* Each stroke made her shake, shiver. Her nerves were singing with sensation, the fullness and friction of him deep inside. His fingers dug into her waist, his other hand still pressed over her lips. She kissed his palm, unthinking.

"Ohhh," he groaned in a low voice that she felt in her chest, her stomach. "I've got you. Does it feel good? Isn't this what you wanted, what you needed all along?"

She could only sob. She was way too far gone to answer. Her cries rose in volume the closer she came to orgasm. Each stroke brought her closer, closer still. Each stroke was fulfillment and revelation. She started to vibrate, to shake and pant against his hand. He let her go and reached down, sliding his fingers between her pussy lips. She bucked back against him, shaking her head. No, it was impossible. No, sex couldn't possibly feel this good. Sex couldn't possibly be like this, a living dream killing her and bringing her back to life. She was vaguely aware of him nuzzling her, kissing and nibbling her shoulder, soft black hair against her cheek. Warm lips tracing down her temple. His fingers stroked her with a dexterity that was unknown to her. A new world of arousal coiled in her belly and then, when she thought she would die, the arousal unwound in a shattering arc. He held her while she fell apart in his arms, gripped by the most intense orgasm she'd ever experienced. Her body tensed, her pelvis pulsed and bucked as the pleasure overtook her. She felt spent, totally emptied out from the force of it. He thrust in her a few more times, finding his own release with a guttural groan against her ear. They both went still, gasping for breath. He didn't pull out, only pressed closer against her. She realized then that her hands were still on the wall on either side of her head.

"Are you okay?" he breathed against her ear.

"No," she gasped. "No, no...no..."
No, she was shocked. She was annihilated.
She was not okay at all.

Okay, so maybe he'd come on a little strong, Ryan thought to himself as he held her. Maybe he'd gone a little further than he'd originally intended. But god, she'd really needed a spanking. She'd looked up at him with that lost, pleading look, the look subs got when they were out of control, when they needed tending. He had tended her all right. And after that, well, she'd really needed to be fucked.

"Are you okay?" he asked her again a moment later while he did up his jeans. She turned and looked at him as if to say *are you nuts?* He tried to kiss her but she turned her head away.

"No."

"Why not?"

He ran his hand up her thigh, pulling her panties back up, smoothing her skirt down over her ass, caressing those gorgeous scarlet globes one last time. She was still trembling and her legs were shaky. He cupped her face in his hands, trying to catch her gaze.

"Look at me."

"No," she moaned.

"I don't like to be told no. What's wrong?"

"What's wrong? What do you think is wrong? How can you ask me that?"

"Kat, I think something is very right between us. I don't think anything's wrong at all." He finally got her to look up at him, only to find the walls in place again.

"I have to go," she said, pushing at him. "You really have to let me go now. Right now."

Poor little girl. He knew he'd freaked her out and he understood the agitation she felt. He knew he needed to give her space and time to think about things. Hell, he needed to do some thinking himself, but he had made one decision for sure. Ekaterina Argounov was worth the trouble after all.

"Okay," he said. "I'll let you go, but I'm walking you to the door. You're leaving here alone tonight."

She fussed with her skirt, checking herself all over as if someone might be able to tell from something besides her shell-shocked expression what had just gone on. He leaned to kiss her again before he unlocked the door.

She looked up at him. "No—"

He muffled her refusal by pressing a soft kiss to her lips.

"Don't," she warned him.

He held his tongue. He had and he would and he was going to again. Not right now. He wouldn't push it now while she was freaked-out and skittish. She had every reason in the world to be scared. For fuck's sake, he was scared too. He had planned to bring her back here, give her a good talking-to in private and send her out of his life for good. He wasn't sure when those plans changed, but they had changed drastically and irrevocably. She was going to be his. His mind was made up.

He led her through the nightclub to the door, his hand still wrapped around her elbow.

"Let go of me," she said, looking around them.

"Nobody knows, you know."

"I don't care."

At the door, out in the cool night air, he kissed her again, but she shied away so his lips pressed beneath her earlobe.

"I'm going to call you tomorrow."

"I won't be home," she said, taking off down the street.

"I bet you will," he replied to her retreating back. God, that beautiful ass. It was going to haunt him until he had it in his hands again. Her reactions to him had been amazing. She had responded to his touch like a finely tuned instrument.

Behind her walls, beneath her reserve, she was vibrating with passion. More importantly, she took to submission like a natural. He couldn't wait to Dom her again, really train her up to the good stuff.

She didn't make it easy for him, though, just as he'd suspected. She didn't answer any of his nightly calls to the Argounov household the following week and she didn't return to the club. No matter — he had a secret weapon. He dialed the Argounov number, this time during the day while Kat was at work. "Hullo?" came the strident voice he remembered.

"Mrs. Argounov," he said in his most polite, eligible-bachelor tone, "this is Ryan McCarthy, Kat's friend from the hospital. I'm so sorry I haven't called before now. I'd love to come to that dinner you offered and meet Kat's father. How is Kat, anyway?"

He could hear the excitement in her voice when she replied, "Oh, Dr. Ryan McCarthy! Katya is doing just fine. How wonderful you call here. You come see her and have dinner with us. This is great!"

"I'd love to surprise her. Just show up to dinner, you know? Kind of blow her mind?"

"Okay, yes." Her mother chuckled conspiratorially. "Blow the mind. Yes, that is a good idea. You come tomorrow night and Katyusha, she will be surprised."

Ryan thought surprised might be an understatement. But he was a goal-driven person and now he had a goal. He sat down and absently started folding cranes, lost in thoughts of thick dark curls, deep green eyes and Kat's skin against his cheek.

* * * * *

Nope. Surprised wasn't the best word for what Kat seemed to be feeling when he showed up at the Argounov home the next night. Elena pulled him in, enveloping him in a smothering hug. Over Elena's shoulder, Kat pinned him with a murderous glare.

"Ekaterina," Elena snapped. "Come and greet your visitor. Look! Look who has come."

"I see him," Kat said.

"Well, come give a hug to him. This man who help you when you banged your head very bad. He helped you."

Helped her, thought Ryan. *And spanked her and fucked her silly in a storage closet last week.*

"Come, come greet him," Elena crowed, pushing Ryan toward her. "She is looking well, no, Ryan?" She said it like Ry-*ann*. "Completely her old self."

He gave Kat a huge smile. "Ekaterina. You do look great. Really, completely wonderful." He hugged her, holding her close and whispered in her ear, "Don't grind your teeth."

"You're kidding me, right?" she whispered back. "You're here for dinner? Very nice."

"Yes, it was very nice of your mother to invite me. It was terribly rude of me to wait so long."

"Katya, go," interrupted Elena. "Go in the kitchen and help your sisters. I introduce Dr. Ryan McCarthy to your father. He has wanted to meet Dr. Ryan and say thank you."

"Yes, we know he's a doctor already, Mama," Kat muttered before turning on her heel to obey. She disappeared into the back of the home, her family's wonderful home that was crowded, cluttered and absolutely resonant with life. Ryan waded through playing children and toys to where Kat's father sat in the TV room off the living room.

"Dmitri! Dmitri!" Elena said briskly.

The thin, gray-haired man looked up at Ryan with a confused gaze as Elena rousted him from his easy chair.

"Here is the man, this one, Dr. Ryan McCarthy. He is the one who has saved your daughter's life."

"Well," Ryan said, "I just tried to stop the bleeding and got her to the hospital. I wouldn't exactly say I saved her life—"

"Oh, I do thank you," Kat's father interrupted, clasping him in a smothering embrace. For an older, somewhat delicate-looking man, his grip was surprisingly strong. "You have saved my princess. I owe you my life. My many thanks are yours," he said, backing away with some effusive bows. His English was flawless and unaccented, if somewhat clipped.

"It was my pleasure to come to her assistance," Ryan replied, perhaps a little formally. The whole event here, his royal reception, left him feeling like nothing less than a prince. He was seated later, of course, at the head of the table in a place of honor with Kat at his right side. Too bad the princess hated his guts.

Kat was silent throughout the meal, one of the most delicious meals Ryan had ever had the pleasure of eating. Her sisters cooed over their children and listened while Elena grilled him on every aspect of his life and Dmitri nodded from the other end of the table. But Kat just sat beside him in silence, stewing and blushing alternately, which charmed him no end. After dinner Elena insisted on reading his fortune, and he was happy to play along. With the whole family looking on, she prophesied a long life and much happiness for him, including many children with the love of his life whose description sounded suspiciously similar to her daughter.

All of this seemed to pain Kat terribly. He could have said, *oh, it's getting late, I'd better go*, but he didn't. It was too fun watching her squirm. And he needed to find some time alone with her before he left because they needed to talk. She disappeared into the kitchen for as long as she was able, but eventually she escaped upstairs. He caught her coming out of the bathroom. She gasped as he took her in his arms.

"Your family is wonderful, do you know that?" he said against her cheek.

She gave a humorless laugh, the smile not quite touching her face. "Is that what you really think?"

"They are. Warm, wonderful. You don't understand how lucky you are."

She pulled away from him. "Why are you here?"

"Where is your bedroom?"

"No boys are allowed upstairs."

"This won't take long. Your bedroom," he repeated.

"I share a bedroom."

"I don't care. Where is it?"

She led him down the hall with a sigh, into a tiny room with a twin bed on one wall and bunk beds on the other. He locked the door.

Her halfhearted *no* was silenced by his kiss. He touched her breasts and caressed her ass, enjoying the feel of her again after craving her so badly. His hands were all over her. He couldn't touch her enough.

"No, no..." she sighed, shaking her head against his neck.

"Yes."

He started undoing his pants. He was going to fuck her. He wished he had time for more, to have her suck him, to bury his face between her legs, but she shared this bedroom, obviously, and her parents were downstairs. He rolled on a condom from his pocket and hiked up her skirt.

"No," she moaned, even as she locked her legs around his waist and arched against him.

"I don't think that word means what you think it means," he said, lowering her onto his cock. He pulled her arms up around his shoulders and then cradled her ass in his hands, squeezing it, kneading it, thrusting in her hard. His hand snaked under her shirt to pinch her nipples through the sheer lacy material of her bra. Soon enough, predictably, her sighs of "no" turned to pleas for satisfaction. *Please, Ryan, please. Please, please, now!*

"Look at me," he ordered when she was getting close. She ignored him, her legs gripping him even tighter. "Look at me,

Kat," he insisted, nuzzling her face up to his. "Come for me. I'll hold you, Kat. Come for me now. I won't let you go." He held her, feeling her tense and shudder and watched the climax seize her. The erotic jerking of her body triggered his own orgasm. He came hard, pulsing explosive pleasure, joining her in her release. Fortunately he had the presence of mind to clamp his palm over her mouth to muffle her cries.

She struggled to get away as soon as she came back to her senses and he let her go with a sigh. She pulled at her skirt, rearranging herself with sharp, jerky tugs.

"You need to stop doing that," she hissed at him.

"I can't."

"Yes, you can. You just don't want to."

"I wouldn't have done this, come here to your house, if you hadn't run away from me. Why didn't you come to the club last night?"

"You said if I came to that club I couldn't act like a whore." She flipped her hair back, challenging him. "And I love to act like a whore, so I went somewhere else."

"Kat," he warned. "Watch the way you speak to me."

"Why? Are you going to spank me again?"

"I might. You'd like it if I did."

"No, I wouldn't."

"Yes, you would. You need it, I think."

She rolled her eyes, turning away from him. "We need to go downstairs. She'll come after us."

He knew she meant Elena, and he was fairly sure she wouldn't, but he followed Kat as she tore down the stairs. She took shelter in the kitchen again, only to have Elena yell for her to bring coffee and cake to her guest.

"He's not my guest, he's your guest," she muttered under her breath. She offered coffee and Russian teacakes on a tray that he had a feeling she would rather have flung in his face. He took pity on her then and made his excuses. He'd accomplished what he'd come to do. She knew now that she wanted him every bit as much as he wanted her, and that avoiding him was pointless. He said his goodbyes, finding himself showered again with hugs and kisses from Elena and Dmitri. He shook the hands of all the husbands and the many sisters he still couldn't tell apart and even fielded a few messy kisses from children of all sizes.

"You will come back again soon, yes?" asked Elena.

"Yes," he said. "I can't wait to come back again. I had a wonderful time."

"Ekaterina," Elena said, "you walk Ryan to the door and say good night."

"Yes, Mama," she answered through gritted teeth.

At the door Ryan kissed her again, even though he knew she hated it.

"I'll call you tomorrow."

"I won't answer."

"If you don't return my calls, if you don't come to the club, I'll be back here again in a week. Your mother loves me. I could eat dinner here every night if I wanted."

"Okay, okay. Fine. I'll come to the club. I'll come on Friday."

"And go out with me after."

"After closing? That's too late."

"The storage room then."

"Okay, fine," she groaned. "God, why are you doing this?"

"Why do you think? I'll see you Friday night, Ekaterina."

"My name is Kat," she corrected with a frown.

"Your name, Ekaterina Argounov, is whatever I want it to be. I'll see you Friday night."

Chapter Four

Ryan went home that night feeling happy and optimistic. Kat's family was great, full of energy and life. There had to be hope for his dour princess and he planned to make her smile if it killed him.

Make her smile and make her do a lot of other things too, things that gave him massive hard-ons when he thought about them too long. His Dominant radar hadn't failed him. She was a submissive all right, just in need of some training and a lot of unconditional love. He began making plans for her, plans for them. He wanted, first, to introduce her to the Dom/sub lifestyle and then he'd try to iron out her mental issues and her self-destructive drive. He imagined himself as a modern-day Pygmalion. He would sculpt her into a work of art, bring her to life. She would be his creation.

If she would cooperate, that was.

Like everything else about her, her relationship with him was ambivalent. She wanted him to take her, then afterward resented being taken. She found fulfillment and then pushed him away. She let him see the lost, flailing girl behind her gaze, but only for a moment before she hid again. He discovered at dinner that she was a translator, that she spent her days transforming English text into Russian. He would need to do the same magic—translate troubled Kat into his lovely Ekaterina. Translate her scowls into smiles.

He sat down to look over some notes, nursing a cup of coffee. He felt tired but invigorated. Soon his mind drifted into more whimsical fantasies. Pretty Ekaterina, the surgeon's wife. She could bring him coffee every night while he went over his medical notes. He would keep her dressed in nothing but a collar and cuffs. Afterward, he could melt away the stress of the day with her. Hell, with what he made she wouldn't even need to work. She could just stay at home and be his sex kitten, his sub. Their relationship would be based on power. His power over her and her willing agreement to submit to that power. And then, perhaps, marriage...children...

But not yet. For now, he needed to concentrate on making her his sub. His obedient, beautiful, pliant, emotionally available sub. His job entailed long hours, a lot of pressure and tension and she would provide a welcome outlet from the stress, although there was a hell of a lot he'd have to teach her to get there. She had a sassy streak a mile wide, not to mention a serious lack of confidence and a hiding problem. No matter. All of that paled in comparison to how aroused she got when he gave her orders, the way she'd reacted to his discipline, the way she moaned and turned to fire when they fucked. He had high hopes for her. When he was done shaping her she would be his prize, all the more special because he'd trained her himself.

He'd been with a lot of subs, trained a lot of girls the way he wanted them and been with a lot already trained, but they'd never fired him up half as much as Kat. Something had coalesced between them that night in the storage room. He knew it. She knew it. The difference was, she still fought it. Oh well, she'd see soon enough.

But he had notes to work on and phone calls to make and it was already late. He would let her simmer until Friday. Friday, he'd spank her again.

Friday arrived, though, and Kat wasn't at the club as he'd told her to be. *You said if I came to that club I couldn't act like a whore. And I love to act like a whore.* She was testing him. Common sub behavior. Would she dare pick up a guy somewhere else? There was no fucking chance he would allow that. He left Masquerade and checked a few other clubs where he thought she might be. Finally, he went to her house and sat on the stoop to wait for her to show up. It was a clear night, pleasant waiting weather at least. But if there was some stupid, drunk guy with her, he was in for the greeting of his life.

Ryan didn't wait long. Just after midnight he saw her come walking down the block. Walking alone in her short little skirt, her tight sweater, her slut heels. She had walked from the club district here to Brighton all by herself. He was going to kill her. She slowed when she noticed him, too far away to see who he was.

Yes, you little fool. I could be a murderer or a rapist sitting here waiting for you.

She looked a little scared to find a strange guy blocking the way, but even more scared when she saw who he was. She turned on her heel and started to walk back in the other direction.

"No. Just...no. Go away," she said when he fell into step beside her.

"I'm not going away. You're a smart girl. You should have figured that out by now. Anyway, you don't want me to. Not really."

Her heels click, click, clicked on the sidewalk and she wrapped her arms around her waist. "I'm tired. I've been out dancing. I just want you to leave me alone."

"Did you walk home from the clubs by yourself or are you coming from someone's house?" he asked as calmly as he was able.

"Wouldn't you like to know?"

He stopped her with a firm hand on her arm. "Yes, I would like to know and you're going to tell me. Were you with someone else tonight?"

"Not that it's any of your business, but no, I wasn't," she said, trying to pull away.

"You aren't coming from someone else's bed?"

"Let go of me or I will scream bloody murder until somebody comes."

He released her and she started to walk again. He took her hand. She tried to pull it away the second he did.

"Just let me hold your hand," he said.

"I don't want to hold your fucking hand." They struggled like two children thumb-wrestling.

"Cut it out! Jesus, you plague me, Kat. Just—" He finally trapped her rigid hand in his.

"You have an annoying habit of manhandling me."

"And you have an annoying habit of irritating me." She was silent but she stopped pulling her hand from his. "Why do you try so hard to avoid me? What have I done?"

"How can you ask that? Do you remember at all pulling me into that storeroom and spanking me and fucking me against the door? Or fucking me in my parents' own house while they all sat downstairs—"

"Yes, and I remember you enjoying both episodes immensely. I remember you falling apart in my arms." She looked furious that she couldn't refute his words but she bit back any false denials.

"So maybe I did. So what? It's still wrong, it's still—"

"What?"

"I don't know. Perverted."

"Like you."

"I am not a pervert. You are."

He sighed. "We both are, Kat. Don't you realize that? That's why things get so hot when we're together. We both have something the other needs."

"I need you to leave me alone."

"Let's just take that off the table. I'm not going to leave you alone because I don't think you want me to. I think you say the exact opposite of what you feel as often as possible. Why do you do that?"

She stood facing him, her hands in fists at her side. Her expression was one of desperation. The angry shrew of the moment before had transformed into his lost girl, conflicted as ever. Her shoulders slumped and the tension in her face unwound, letting the mask fall away just for a moment. He tilted her face up to see green eyes gazing back at him with a frown.

"You know, Kat, this isn't as scary as you're making it."

She pulled away from him, cool and wary again. "You don't understand. You think you do, but you don't understand how this feels to me. I'm really not into this stuff."

"What 'stuff'?"

"Relationships."

"Why? You had a relationship that ended badly?"

"I just...don't like relationships."

"You've never been in a relationship at all?" She crossed her arms over her chest, pouting hard. He gazed at her in disbelief. "You haven't, have you?"

"It's none of your business."

"That means no."

"Fine. No, I haven't. Like I said, I'm not relationship material, and to be honest I wouldn't get into a relationship with you anyway."

"Why not?"

"Because I have a feeling you wouldn't be easy to live with."

Well. She hit close to the truth on that.

* * * * *

Kat wasn't sure how they ended up at the all-night diner. He had a way of getting her to do things she had no intention of doing. She slouched in the booth across from him in her skimpy black club clothes, looking around at all the drunk, happy people. That might have been her if she hadn't come home early and fallen into his clutches. But she'd come home because all she could think about was how bad she craved his fucking clutches, damn it.

She scowled over at him as the waitress poured their coffee, then busied herself emptying four packets of sugar and two shots of cream into her mug. He sighed when she reached for the fifth packet, resting his head on his hand. Was that supposed to impress her, his disapproving sigh? Of course Mr. Perfect drank his decaf black.

He looked around as she stirred her sugary concoction. She slid him a look from under her lashes. Lord. She thought by now she would be inured to his masculine perfection, but she was still taken aback by his sculpted arms, the strength in his shoulders. She was fascinated by the authority he exuded with nothing more than a glance or subtle movement. He was so intelligent, so important. A surgeon. Why was she sitting here with him? Good lord, he'd fucked her brains out twice already. Here in the brightly lit diner, sitting across from him, the realization blew her away.

He wore a white tee, simple but devastating when paired with his perfect biceps and pecs. His face had a symmetry that somehow remained handsome no matter his expression. He looked handsome when he was angry, he looked handsome when he was mild, and when he smiled at her...*damn*. She noticed all the other ladies in the diner casting looks at him. Some of the guys too.

But his annoying psychoanalysis unnerved her. *I think you say the exact opposite of what you feel as often as possible.* It was true. He had totally pegged her and it freaked her out. Unlike all the other men she collected and discarded like trading cards, he alone seemed to understand the unhappiness that dogged her. Which is exactly why she couldn't bear to be in a relationship with him.

"Okay, Kat," he said, leaning back with a sigh. "I'm going to talk, but you have to listen. You have to give this some thought. I know you. You're going to close your mind to whatever I have to say. Try not to do that this time, for once."

"You're so irritating."

"And the smart mouth—first things first. It's got to go."

"I like my smart mouth, and you have no right to tell me what to do."

The waitress appeared before he could respond to that with anything more than a frown. He ordered first, an egg-white omelet with peppers and mushrooms. She barely restrained herself from making a gagging sound. "I'll have a bacon and cheese omelet with a double order of hash browns on the side," Kat said. He shook his head before she even finished.

"I'm afraid I can't let you order that."

She looked over at him, her mouth dropping open. "What?"

"I care about you too much to let you eat that. No. Order something else."

"Are you fucking kidding me?"

He looked over at the waitress with a patient smile. "If you could just give us a minute."

She smiled and sashayed away, obviously under his spell. His charm might work on her, but not on Kat. She glared over at him. "Who the hell do you think you are?"

"Now, Kat—"

"Are you seriously going to tell me what I can and cannot eat? Seriously? I am not fat."

"I never said you were fat. You're actually a little on the thin side in my opinion. But I'm curious what your arteries look like. Or your intestines for that matter."

"Oh god," she groaned, clapping her hands over her ears. "Please stop."

"I'm only suggesting you order something a little healthier. Take care of your body. You've already put an entire day's worth of sugar in your coffee."

"An entire day's worth? An hour's worth, maybe. I like sugar."

"You clearly like grease and nitrates too. But you'd feel better if you ordered something more nutritious, like some proteins and fruit."

"You can take your proteins and fruit and shove them up your fucking—"

"Kat. Language. Please."

Language? Jesus. She stood up, intent on flouncing out of there, but he put his hand over hers, firm pressure and a squeeze.

"Sit down. Sit down or I'll make a scene."

She looked in his dark eyes and saw something there besides the disapproving asshole. A spark that promised mayhem, a mischievous glint. A challenge. She sank back into the booth. The waitress returned and Ryan smiled up at her, handing over the menus.

"She'll have a whole-grain English muffin with fat-free cream cheese and a fresh fruit platter."

"Strawberries and melons okay?" the waitress asked.

"I hate melons," Kat muttered under her breath.

The waitress barely glanced at her, just noted Ryan's approving nod and bustled away. He turned back to Kat.

"Trust me. You'll feel so much better when you eat something healthy."

"Trust me. You just so ruined your chances with me."

He didn't look too worried. She watched him tear a square out of the paper placemat in front of him and start folding it into some kind of shape. "A relationship with me would do you good," he said. "A world of good, if you want my opinion."

"What if I don't want your opinion? What if I don't want to have a relationship with you? Especially when I can't order what I want?"

His mouth twitched a little, a small arrogant smile.

"I think you'd put up with just about anything if I would only spank you again."

Damn it. Was she that transparent? She was obsessed with the thought. She'd thought of little else since the night they'd had their little session in the storage room, and even now, sitting across from him, she felt short of breath. *Touch me, fuck me, lecture me, spank me. Just do anything, anything to me.*

She'd been so stunned and appalled by what he'd done to her that night she had fled in a panic. Actually, it wasn't him she was stunned and appalled by... It was herself. She had been a more than willing participant — in fact she'd completely lost her mind under his hands. When he'd told her he was going to spank her, when he glared at her with those stern, knowing eyes, her clit had caught fire. *You are going to stand there, Ekaterina, and I am going to spank your ass for these crazy choices you make.* She'd repeated it to herself a thousand times since then, remembered the stern tenor of his voice, his exacting tone. Every time he spoke to her now she responded sexually, just as sexually as she'd responded that night.

After she'd left him she had gone home, run upstairs to her room and, finding her nieces asleep there, had run into the bathroom instead and masturbated three times to orgasm before she could think straight again. She had slept and dreamed of him all night, the touch of his fingertips pressing her to the door, the obscenely sexy sound of him unbuckling his belt. She ached. She craved him with an intensity that scared her.

Not good, she told herself. Feelings this intense were too dangerous.

She had gone out of her way to avoid him, staying away from the club, not answering his calls. She felt it was better to just never see him again, to forget her experience in the closet and the tidal wave of desire it had unleashed. But then he had shown up for dinner with that smug smile and basked in the thanks of her family while she squirmed beside him in hot anger and lust. She had tried so hard to avoid him, fought herself so hard to just stay away, and there he was again. When he'd lifted her up in his arms she was more than happy to have him take her...but now...now...

He was looking at her as if this was going to be a whole lot more complicated than that. He handed her the folded placemat critter with a look of gravity and she turned it around in her hands.

"What is this? A monkey?"

He tsked. "A crane."

"What's a crane anyway? Are they like flamingos?"

"Cranes are among the most honored and mythologized creatures in the world."

"Mythologized? Is that even a word?"

"Would you like to wager on it?"

Kat looked up at his devilish grin and shifted. "Uh, no. I'm not going to wager against the genius." She looked back at the origami figure, touched the wide pointed wings and traced the narrow head. "It's neat that you can do this," she finally said.

"I can show you how if you want."

"No. I don't want."

"The Japanese consider the crane an omen of fortune and happiness. They believe that folding one thousand origami cranes can earn you a wish."

She looked up at the tone in his voice. "What kind of wish?"

"Any kind of wish. What do you wish for?"

Happiness. Security. You. "Nothing. It doesn't matter anyway. It's just paper. It doesn't mean anything."

"Doesn't it? My medical license is just paper."

"But that's not just paper. That's all your expertise and knowledge and what it took to get there."

"Yes, and so is this. It takes a long time and a lot of dedication to fold a thousand cranes."

"Getting what you want has nothing to do with cranes," she said stubbornly. She felt the strangest urge to cry. She looked around the diner to distract herself and was relieved to see the waitress approaching with their food. Kat shoved the crane to the side as the waitress put the plates down between them. As unappetizing as it looked, she dug into the fruit plate, picking the strawberries out from the unwanted melon.

"What does it have to do with then?" he asked.

She looked up in surprise. "What?"

"Getting what you want. What does it have to do with, if not with cranes?"

"Is that a trick question? Are you trying to mess with me? Why don't you just eat your whole-grain omelet or whatever crap you ordered?"

"It's not a trick question and I'm not trying to do anything to you except get to know you better. See what makes you tick."

She looked at the gelatinous cream cheese on her English muffin and took a tentative bite. Ugh, the fat-free stuff was disgusting. The small morsel lodged in her throat. She closed her eyes, feeling overwhelmed, trapped and emotional. "I don't even know what makes me tick," she said in a tight voice.

"Maybe if you knew you wouldn't be so unhappy."

She frowned down at her coffee, at the swirly patterns in the creamy film on top. She took a sip, washing down the offending muffin. "I'm not unhappy. I'm just a really private person. I always have been."

"Private? Or lonely?"

"I don't trust people. I don't trust—look—I mean—"

"You're an unhappy person."

She scowled at him. "Simplify much? You don't understand me because you aren't like me."

"Then explain to me. How can I help?"

"I don't want your help. You helped me quite enough. Anyway, why do you care?"

"Why do you think I care?" His gaze captured hers. That traitorous part of her twisted and flailed to be heard. She pressed her legs together.

"I really don't know and I don't want to know."

He lowered his voice and leaned closer across the table.

"Kat, have you ever heard of something called Dominance and submission?"

Had she ever heard of it? Ever since their interlude the week before, she'd browsed every D/s site she could find. Not that she would admit it to him. She shrugged, pretending nonchalance. "I know a little about it. A few things."

"What do you know about it?"

"I know you're into it. That it's like...spanking...bondage...leather...that kind of stuff."

"Sure, that's part of it, but it's a whole lot more complicated than that."

"Like how complicated?"

"Sometimes extremely complicated and sometimes not very complicated at all. It depends. When things fall into place between people it can be very simple. If people want complementary things from each other it works like a dream."

"How do you know? You've done it, I guess?"

"Yes. Had some good relationships and some bad. But I've never felt for any sub the way I feel for you."

"I'm not a sub," she said at once, thinking about the women on the kink sites, trussed and gagged. "I'm not into that weirdo stuff."

"I think you are. You want to be controlled, taken care of. And I'd like to do the controlling. You need someone to settle you down, to make you feel safe. You want someone to tell you what to do, someone who knows what's best for you. You want someone to sweep you up and hold you tight."

How did he know that? He was so completely right but she was still shaking her head in denial, unwilling to accept that her longtime romantic desires translated, somehow, into submission to a man.

"Listen, I know it's new and different to you," he went on, his face a picture of empathy. "I know it's hard to accept at first. You think it will make you weak and helpless when you submit to me."

"It does make me feel weak and helpless. It did!"

He held up a hand and admonished her quietly. "Remember, I asked you to think first, not just to react. Just think about what I'm saying."

"Okay," she muttered. "Explain to me the specifics of how it will benefit me to become your slave."

"Slave? I never said anything about you being a slave."

"I thought that's what it was all about. On those websites—" She stopped, blushing.

He grinned at her. "Been cruising websites? Which ones?"

She named a few of the bigger ones and his smile widened.

"Listen, most of those sites are over the top. They're porn. Fantasy. I want a sub, not a slave. I'm not going to keep you collared and chained to the bed. You'll live your own life as you always have. But you'll also have me. More of what you had in the storage room. I don't think that would be a really great hardship for you."

She blushed scarlet, looking down at her hands. The conversation had left her speechless. She choked down another bite of the English muffin, chasing it with another deep swig of coffee.

"There's nothing wrong with liking it, Kat. With wanting it."

She shook her head. She didn't like it. She didn't want it... Did she?

She did. Why did she want it? What was she going to do now that he was offering it to her?

"I'm not sure about this," she said finally. "I'm just not sure. I'm not even that good in bed."

He laughed. "Let me be the judge of that. Anyway, it's not just about the bedroom. Sex. Fucking. I mean, that's a big part of it but not the whole thing. Anyway, whatever I want from you, I'll teach you. I'll train you to be exactly what I want."

I'll train you. She could barely draw breath. The very idea of it was enough to make her almost orgasm where she sat. But what if he wanted really sick stuff from her? Some of the photos she'd seen on the S&M websites left her more disturbed than aroused.

"What you are you thinking?" he asked.

She shrugged. "I just don't know what you'll expect of me. If it will be too much, if I'll want to do what you ask me or if..."

"If it will be too weird?"

"Yes."

"Well, what would be too weird for you?"

"I don't know," she said, sounding as conflicted as she felt. "I don't know too much about it. I didn't like some of what I saw."

"On those websites? I don't want you on those anymore, do you understand? Tell me what you saw that so upset you."

"I don't know... People hurting people... Burning them with wax, cutting them... Sticking them with needles. Fucking them up with all this hardware."

"Jesus, Kat," he said with a smile. "Going right for the hard-core. Leave it to you. What else?"

"I don't want to be made to look ugly, put in masks or gags or... You know... Have to get weird piercings or be... Marked. Scarred." She shuddered. "How hard will you hit me. Will you ever...?" She couldn't finish the thought.

"Oh, Kat," he said with a sigh. "I wish you hadn't gone to those sites at all. Look, I want to control and discipline you, not disfigure you. Part of being in a D/s relationship is negotiating. You can have hard limits, things you won't even consider. Soft limits, things you're curious about. Things you really do want that you can tell me about. Partners work it all out."

"You won't leave marks on me?"

"I won't leave any marks that won't fade. But I'll mark you, yes. I like doing that. I marked you that night at the club, you remember."

Yes, she remembered. She'd stared at those marks, caressed them, masturbated over them for two days. She'd been disappointed when they started to fade.

"I promise you, it won't ever be too much," he said. "We'll have agreements on how far to go. We'll use safewords."

"Safewords?"

"Yes, we'll have a safeword that will stop me when you feel I'm going too far. I'm not into making you miserable. I won't force you to do anything you really don't want to do."

"But I know you'll want more than I do.

He chuckled. "I don't think you know how much you want yet. How much you'll love what I'm going to do to you. You don't have any idea yet, but you'll see. You'll want much more than you think."

"So what... How much... How hard...?" Her imagination was stuck in overdrive. She was sure her unease was reflected in the expression on her face.

He took her hand across the table. "Kat, I'm not really into pushing envelopes. Would you like to know what I'd expect from you, more or less? In general terms, to soothe your nerves?"

"Yes," she breathed on a sigh.

"Obedience and submission."

"That's it?"

"That comprises a lot of things. You'll have a lot to learn. Sometimes things will be stringent, sometimes relaxed. You'll figure it out. You'll come to understand exactly what I want and when, and you'll get good at giving it to me."

"Because if I don't..."

"I'll punish you. Real punishment. Discipline. That's part of the dynamic, the turn-on. For me and for you."

She blushed because what he said was true. It would turn her on terribly for him to discipline her, no matter how much it hurt. She looked up at him. He must have known that her panties, by now, were soaked.

"All of this...you know... I don't know. My mother says I should be trying to find a husband, settle down and have kids."

"Hmm. Probably."

"That's what all my sisters have done."

"I don't think you're much like your sisters. I don't think you want to be. I think that's why life is so hard for you."

"So..." she said slowly, the wheels turning. She had to admit she was actually considering his suggestions. But she thought he was overestimating how happy he'd be with her. "Here's the thing. I'm not really... I don't... I've only just had sex, you know, regular sex. I'm not really good at...the extra stuff."

"Anal sex?"

The casual way he said it made blood rush to her face. "Yeah. Or even stuff like...blowjobs."

She fell silent. He looked shocked.

"All those guys you went home with, you never...?"

"I just had them fuck me and then I left."

"No foreplay, no playing around?"

"Sometimes they wanted to go down on me, but I didn't want them to, and I've never even tried to give a blowjob," she admitted, not quite able to meet his eyes. "I mean, why would I? I didn't like them anyway. We never even kissed."

He made a soft sound. "I see now. You took what you wanted. You used them. Well, Kat, it will be different with me."

She swallowed nervously. "Yes, I'm sensing that. If you even still want me now that I've told you I'm not good in bed."

"You let me worry about that. I have no doubt I can train you to satisfy me, if you're willing to be trained." He leaned his elbows on the table, looked right at her with a serious expression on his face. "So are you willing or not?"

"Willing to what?"

"Give it a try. Sexual training. Submission and obedience."

She drew in her breath. *Yes, yes, I want to start training this instant.*

"If I say yes, then what happens?" she asked, her heart in her throat.

"If you say yes then you come to my place tomorrow night for Lesson Number One."

"Lesson Number One?"

"I think it's high time, Kat, that you learned to suck cock."

* * * * *

He took her out to dinner first. He didn't want her to mistake their fledgling relationship for one of the emotionless hookups she was used to, especially since they were going to be having a lot of sex. Ryan always had a lot of sex but he was after more here. There was more at stake.

He texted her and told her to be ready at seven. He'd made reservations at an intimate gourmet restaurant near his place in Cambridge. He wasn't on call this weekend so there was no chance of the seduction being interrupted. And he did plan a seduction. A girl didn't reach the age of twenty-eight completely blowjob-free if she felt positive about them. He hoped he could change her mind.

When he arrived to pick her up she wasn't quite ready, so he made small talk with Elena and Dmitri and watched the sisters pass around the fussy baby. Yuri or Sergei or something. He could never keep the names straight. If they were English names he could have, but they were names like Rada and Varvara and Zinaida, and then their husbands would call them pet names like Radya and Varvusha and Zinoushka until he was completely lost and content to just soak up the family vibe. He would love for his children to grow up with an extended family like Kat's. A doting grandma like Elena, ten smiling aunties and uncles coming and going and too many cousins to count. He was just smiling over what his own parents' reaction might be to the bedlam in the Argounov household when she came down the stairs.

The noise and activity around him continued but he stopped and stared. She was wearing a gorgeous, fitted dress with embroidery, and her hair was up in a loose chignon with tendrils of curls falling down in spirals against her face. She was beautifully made-up, with deep red lips that drew his gaze and made him think terribly inappropriate thoughts there in the living room of her parents' home.

He met her at the bottom of the stairs and took her hand. "You look gorgeous," he whispered. As usual, she shied away when he brushed a kiss against her cheek. She smelled like flowers and vanilla sugar. He barely restrained himself from licking her in front of her mother and father.

"Thank you. You're looking pretty good yourself."

He looked down at his crisp white shirt and navy jacket. Just another male clod ready to sacrifice himself at the altar of feminine beauty and allure.

"Come on, let's go. We have reservations."

At the restaurant, she sat stiffly across from him. It was an upscale place, the type with a lot of silverware and glassware on the table and no prices on the menu. She toyed with her napkin in her lap, looking almost mournful.

"You know, you didn't have to do this," she said.

"Do what?"

"Bring me here. Drop a lot of money on me."

He frowned, glancing up at her over the menu. "I do what I want with you. That's how D/s relationships work. If I want to bring you to a fancy restaurant and show you off to everyone, I will."

The compliment didn't seem to register. She frowned back at him. "Are you going to tell me what I can and can't eat here too? Or just at diners?"

He didn't rise to the bait, maintaining a fond and relaxed demeanor as he closed his menu. "I believe I'll order for us both."

"What if I don't like what you order?"

"You'll either go hungry or choke it down. But everything is very good here."

She closed her menu and handed it to him with a touch of pique. "I'm sure it is."

He continued to watch her. He could see the internal struggle, the desire to enjoy herself and let him take care of her warring with her desire to protect her independence at all costs. He leaned forward, gazing at her over the candlelight.

"I brought you here to make you feel special. I want you to understand that I'm not just out to use you." The waiter brought wine and Ryan ordered, crusted salmon for himself and citrus chicken for Kat. After the waiter left, he looked back at her. "You should know, Kat, that I won't let you use me either."

"I have no intention of using you."

"Good. We're on the same page then."

"This is just a lot of trouble and expense to go to for a blowjob."

"Kat," he warned.

"Especially when it probably won't be a very good one."

The "probably" encouraged him at least. "We'll see. As much as I'd like to continue talking about the lessons I plan to give you later, it's not appropriate dinner conversation. Let's talk about something else. Like how beautiful your hair looks by candlelight."

"You're a romantic."

"Yes."

"I'm not."

"Do we have anything at all in common, do you think?" he asked in exasperation. "Maybe we should just throw in the towel."

"I'm sorry. I just don't feel comfortable here."

"I know. That's part of why I brought you here. I'll enjoy making you do things you're not quite comfortable with. It's a big part of how I get off."

"Why?"

"It's a power thing. What can I make you do? How far can I push you? What will I do when you balk? Not to mention the fact that when you're off balance, you need me more than when you're in control."

She didn't reply but she was breathing notably faster. She took a small sip of wine and he watched her lick her lips, look sideways and then down. Her neck was beautiful, slender and graceful. She felt frightened but she was trying to hide it. Cornered prey. Beautiful Russian doll. He was wild to have her by the time the waiter brought the check.

Chapter Five
ఴ

On the way to his house after dinner, Kat sat beside him feeling nervous, watching his long, forceful fingers on the gearshift. He pulled up to a neat little two-story colonial and led her to a small porch on the side. She fidgeted while he dug for keys, looking down at the design on the woven welcome mat. She thought his house was kind of smallish, but most Cambridge houses were.

He flipped on the lights when they entered and Kat blinked, looking around. So bland and orderly, sterile like an operating room and so quiet compared to her busy home. Of course, he was just a single guy, while her home was overflowing with way too many people. She turned at the soft touch on the small of her back. He had touched her that same way the first time they spoke up on the balcony. She had never imagined, back then...

"Are you thirsty? Can I get you anything?"

"I'm fine. Could I use your bathroom?"

"Sure." He led her down the hall to the bathroom, which she fully intended to explore and analyze. She shut the door and peed, all the while looking around to see what she could glean. Tidy. Nice sparkling shower stall. He obviously had a maid. She stealthily opened the medicine cabinet. No scary prescription drugs, just condoms and ibuprofen. She closed it silently and looked in the mirror. *Are you ready to do this?* She was somewhat uneasy about all the submissive business. Uneasy and yet curious. And hot.

"Okay?" he asked when she came out.

"Yes, I'm fine."

"Come here."

She walked over to him and he started, without prelude, to take off her clothes. He did it casually, with no words between them, just his dark gaze focused on the task of stripping her. He took off her dress, her shoes, her tights, until she stood trembling in her black bra and panties, and then, after a brief appreciative stare, he took those off too. She reached up to cover herself but he pushed her hands back down.

"Don't. My submissive, my body. I want to see you."

She made a soft noise, of protest or assent, she wasn't sure. She didn't know where to look while he scrutinized her from head to toe.

"Okay," he said at last. "Kneel down here by the sofa, back straight, hands in your lap until I tell you to move."

She did as he asked while he walked around doing various things, checking his mail, going into the bathroom. She heard the shower turn on and still she knelt there as he'd told her to, but at some point she started to tremble. By the time he came out she was shaking with anxiety. He came and sat in front of her on the sofa, totally nude, and lifted her face in his hand.

"What's wrong? Tell me."

"Why did you leave me here?"

"I had things I wanted to do first. You wait where I leave you. That's the deal. Does that upset you?"

"I don't know," she said, and she really didn't know. She wasn't really upset. She was horny, excited, shocked, scared…and frantic. Frantic to do what he wanted, to be what he wanted her to be.

"Just please tell me what to do now, because I don't know what to do. I want to make you happy. I want to be good at this."

He made a soft sound and worked for a moment at her messy chignon. The hair tumbled down and he laced his fingers through her curls, pulling them just a little. He scooted forward, his knees on either side of her so she was face-to-face with his cock. *God. Oh my god.*

"What?" he teased. "You've never seen one before?"

"It's just...big." She shook her head. "That will never fit in my mouth."

He laughed. "It'll fit. Don't look so scared. We've had sex twice already and you survived just fine. Go on, put your hands on it first. Explore it. You'll get to know it well over the next weeks and months."

"But what do you want me to do? What will make you feel good?"

"You obeying me without a lot of questions will make me feel good. Take me in your hands as I asked you to."

She did, gingerly at first. "Cup my balls," he said quietly. "Stroke the shaft. Play with me. Not too gently," he added. She held him in her hands, amazed that he could feel so warm and yet hard and smooth like granite. She had touched cocks before but she'd done it mindlessly, carelessly. Not like now. She focused on his organ, the rigid, upstanding shaft before her and the balls beneath, stroking their textures and contours. He twisted his fingers in her hair, tightening his hold as her touch grew more confident. The dull discomfort of having her hair pulled barely registered over the novelty of exploring his erection.

"Yes, good girl," he murmured, dropping his head back. "That's right. That feels good."

Kat felt a frisson of deeply feminine satisfaction at his exhalation of pleasure. *Good girl.* She was pleasing him. She wanted his exacting instructions, his piercing gaze. She wanted his approval, something she had never sought from a man in her life.

"Hands back in your lap. Part your lips," he said. "Just slightly for now." She lowered her hands and clasped them together in her lap, opening her mouth as he'd directed. Too wide? Not wide enough? She gazed up at him seeking guidance but he was staring at her mouth, his eyes liquid and intent. He slowly caressed her lips with the head of his cock. She remained still, still as a statue. He had promised to teach her. Finally he met her eyes, the muscles in his jaws clenched as if he were in pain. "Listen to me, Kat," he said, stroking her cheek with light fingertips. "It will take practice and effort for you to get skilled at this. What I expect from you now is good intentions. You'll do your best and you'll pretend to enjoy every moment my cock is in your mouth. You can answer me now with 'Yes Sir,' nice and sweet."

"Yes Sir." The formal words felt awkward, but she managed them.

"I want you to get your mouth nice and wet and open it up wide. I want you to take as much of me as you can manage. Okay? Try not to gag. 'Yes Sir' again," he prompted.

"Yes Sir." She was staring at his cock. Now that the moment of truth was here she was feeling a lot less confident. "Are you... Are you going to..."

"Finish in your mouth? Not yet, not until we're tested. But yes, eventually I will and when I do, you'll swallow. Spitting isn't allowed, little one. And you won't just swallow me, you'll savor me. Okay?"

Her clit throbbed at the way he said it. She'd never tasted cum in her life but the idea of it suddenly became totally hot. "Yes Sir."

"Very good. Okay. Open wider." He pushed just the head of his cock into her mouth and she already felt overwhelmed. He was so big. She'd seen porn actresses bobbing their faces up and down on men's cocks, making it look easy. It wasn't easy at all. She felt clumsy and inept. Oops—she'd definitely nicked him with her teeth just then. She waited for criticism but he brushed his fingers over her hair and shifted closer to her. "Wider. You can do it, just try. Just let it slide in and out. Don't fight it."

She tried to relax her mouth. It was getting easier as her mouth got wetter. She finally felt she was getting the hang of it but then he thrust deeper. She gagged and he pulled out, then entered again, carefully inching deeper and deeper with each subsequent stroke so that, very soon, she was taking much more of him than she'd ever expected to manage.

"That's right. You're doing wonderful," he said, caressing the back of her neck. He was barely halfway in. Still, she could tell she was giving him pleasure by the noises he made and the way his hands tightened on her skin. She slid her tongue over his shaft, caressing him with her lips. "Now touch me," he said with a gasp. Words seemed to desert him then. He reached down and brought one of her hands to the lower half of his shaft. She squeezed the base of his cock, caressing what she couldn't handle with her mouth. On pure instinct, she put her other hand on his balls, toyed with and teased them. He groaned. "God, you're a natural." He gave her breathless instructions. *Harder...softer...faster...deeper...* She felt his balls tighten, felt his body grow tense. He put a hand on her shoulder and drew out of her and with a low groan, he climaxed, shooting hot cum on her chest and breasts. She sat still, appalled and yet fascinated. His hand tightened.

"Stay," he said. "Don't move an inch." He let out a sigh and looked down at her. She felt marked, used. She had made him come and he'd come on her. Now he seemed in no hurry to let her wipe it away. He reached out instead and ran a rough fingertip over each of her very hard nipples. The sensation was overwhelming, a hot pang of lust shooting right down to her pussy He brought her to boiling with nothing more than carefully placed touches. She needed to be fucked, right away.

"I guess I should have warned you."

"Warned me?" Her brain was mush. *Fuck me now, please. But oh no, you just came.*

"Warned you," he said, chuckling. "Warned you that I was going to finish all over your chest. Ever had a guy come on your tits before?"

"Um, no."

He got up and produced a box of tissues from a side table, wiping away the semen with firm strokes. "What about your face? Ever get a facial?"

"What?"

"I'll take that as a no." He gazed down at her with an amused smile, tossing the tissues to the side and taking her face in his hands. "That was very good. Excellent, actually. A lot better than I expected. You enjoyed that more than you thought, didn't you?" He stroked behind her ear then brushed some errant tendrils of hair back from her face. He leaned to kiss her, holding her head, thrusting his tongue into her mouth so that she felt her whole body respond. When he drew away she was disappointed that he'd let her go.

"Little Ekaterina," he whispered against her cheek, "does mama wait up for you at home? Can you sleep here tonight?"

"I can't... I mean... I can stay a little while longer but—"

"But the idea of sleeping over terrifies you."

"She'll worry."

"And the idea of sleeping over terrifies you."

"Yes," she sighed. "A little."

"A lot. You're a little liar. That's one habit you'll have to break. Well, come on." He pulled her to her feet and back to his bedroom. It was as spare and practically furnished as the rest of the house, although the bed he nudged her toward looked quite comfortable. He pointed at the expanse of fluffy white comforter and multicolored pillows. "Lie down on your back and spread your legs. Pull up your knees."

She sat on the edge of the bed, about to protest until his look compelled her to lie back. "Spread your legs," he repeated, a little more sternly.

"Why?"

He gave her another look. "Because I told you to. Lie back and open your legs right now, Kat. Don't make me say it again."

"What are you going to do?"

"I'm going to suck on your clit and lick your pussy and you're going to let me do it." He came to her and pushed her knees apart but she fought him, the submission she felt moments before ebbing away.

"No, I don't want that. I really don't. I just don't like it."

He frowned dangerously. "Sometime I'm going to figure out what's going on with that, but not now. I want to taste you and I have no desire to pry your legs apart while you deny me."

"Ryan—"

"Sir."

"Sir, just—okay, here's the thing—" He climbed onto the bed next to her, pressing her back against the sheets. "Please, I just don't—" His fingers crept up her thigh, parted her. God, she couldn't believe how wet she was. He looked at her.

"You want it."

"No."

"Don't tell me no, when all I want is to give you pleasure," he said sharply. "Your body is mine."

"Is it?" she challenged.

"Isn't it? Aren't you my submissive tonight? Isn't that what we talked about?"

"Well, yes—"

"Then open your legs the way I asked."

"Please—"

"What?" he snapped. "Explain—and make it good. You've already earned yourself a spanking with your behavior. So tell me why, Kat? Why can't I?"

"It's too intimate," she said, pleading with her gaze for him to understand. "Please, it's too intimate for me."

"Whether it's too intimate for you or not, it's not going to hurt and it's what I want, so I'm afraid you'll need to submit to this whether you want to or not. And I'll expect you to come for me," he added, noticing her steeling herself.

Whatever. No way was she going to come. He pushed her back and parted her knees with his shoulders. If she really fought him, she knew he would let her up. She wanted him to fuck her, not this. She didn't want this...this intimacy...this attention. She gritted her teeth as he lowered his mouth to her wet slit, teasing it with featherlight touches. *No. You won't like it. Don't like it.*

"God, you're beautiful down here, Kat. Your clit is swollen and wet. That excites me."

She shook her head and swallowed a moan as he licked and sucked at her button, nibbled it a little. She reached down, clutching his shoulders. "Please."

"Is this new to you?" he murmured against her slick folds. "You never let any of them do this? The others?"

"No." She moaned again, twisting under his mouth. "Never."

"So I'm the first one?" he asked, kissing and sucking her with just the right amount of teasing pressure to make heat flare and spread. Against her intentions, she felt desire begin to override her inhibitions. She started to make small, muffled noises of pleasure with each delicious stroke of his teasing tongue. He slid one finger up inside her, practiced control and persistence. *Oh lord, please help me.* "Am I the first one to have you this way?" he asked again.

"Yes," she said. "God, Ryan!"

"Call me Sir."

"God, Sir!" she wailed. He pinned her hips down and licked her all over with intimate, sensual strokes. She bucked and strained under him, her pelvis throbbing, the pressure building until she thought she would die. But she couldn't let go... She just couldn't let go...

"Does that feel good, baby?"

"Yes...S...Sir..." The unfamiliar address was getting a lot easier to use the more horny she was.

"Do you want me to make you come?"

"Yes, please, yes! Please."

"You were so naughty, though, resisting me. I'm not sure that you deserve to come. I think you need to be taught a lesson about who's in charge."

She moaned. She had to come. He had to let her.

"Perhaps I should just stop and send you home for the evening," he said, nibbling on her clit. The anticipation was unbearable. Her whole body was shaking, suffused with urgent need. She was almost sobbing now.

"Please, don't stop. Please, please...Sir!"

It was the "Sir" that did it. He shouldn't have allowed her to come after the way she'd fought him, but she remembered to address him correctly when she was half-insane with desire, and progress like that was rewarded. He thrust a finger back inside her slick wetness, then two, stroking her roughly, fanning the spark inside her to light into flame. He breathed in the sweet musky scent of her, the female essence, hot and wet on his lips and hands. He could feel it when she came. She was so tight, gripping his fingers. Even if he hadn't felt her climax, her drawn-out groan of relief would have given it away. He watched her let go, forget everything but the sensation he was giving her. She was beautiful in the throes of orgasm, like a wild mythological goddess, dark hair and lashes against porcelain skin flushed with passion. He held her down until the shudders subsided, then kissed up her pelvis to her flat tummy, then up between her breasts rising and falling in the aftermath.

"Next time," he whispered into the hollow of her clavicle, "I'll tie you down first."

Her eyes fluttered open, fixed on him and dilated.

He leaned over her with a smug grin. "That wasn't so bad now, was it?"

She launched herself into his arms and he held her tightly. God, she felt so good, so right. The shuttered, defensive girl was gone, replaced by this woman clinging to his neck. She pressed her cheek to his, buried her fingers in his hair. He'd known it would be this way.

"It wasn't bad at all," she finally admitted. "I kind of liked it."

"*Kind of* liked it?"

She giggled at his feigned outrage and he laughed with her, leaning back to take in the vision of her happy and relaxed in his arms. It was a start. It was progress. He sobered, dropping soft kisses on her forehead and then whispering against her lips.

"It wasn't so bad, but you were bad, weren't you?"

He felt her go tense, shiver.

"I'm sorry," she said, pulling away from him a little.

"'I'm sorry, Sir.'"

"I'm sorry, Sir," she corrected with a blush. "I just... I can't explain..."

"Then let me explain to you. You can't balk at intimacy in a relationship like this. Things are going to get a whole lot more intimate than me going down on you. A lot more intimate," he repeated with a warning look.

She looked away, but he drew her gaze back with a soft warning tsk. "I was just afraid, I guess," she said. "This stuff scares me a little."

"I know. I know you're still learning. Let this be a lesson to you. You need to trust me. You need to understand that I'll always want what's best for you. If you decide to fight me on something, you'd better think long and hard about whether it's warranted."

"I will. I promise. From now on."

"I'm sure you will. However, there's still the matter of your punishment."

"Punishment? But...but like you just said... I'm... I'm still learning."

He silenced her protests with a kiss. "Yes, you're still learning. Here's Lesson Number Two. When I feel like punishing you, I will."

She pouted against his lips. "In my opinion, that lesson doesn't seem very fair."

"Lesson Number Three," he said quietly. "Sometimes life with me isn't fair."

He made her stand in front of him and talk first, only because he found it an effective way of both disciplining her and turning her on.

"Eyes up," he snapped when he noticed her gaze dropping for the fourth time to his full-on erection. "You can worry about that later. Answer me. Why are you being punished?"

"Um. For hiding?"

"Yes. For hiding and saying no and generally being an uncooperative little pain. Next time Sir wants to lick your wet little pussy, what are you going to do?"

"Um..." she said, shifting from foot to foot.

"Spread your legs wide and let him do it?"

"Yes Sir."

"What if Sir wants to do something else you don't like? Something you're really terrified of?"

"Um... I have to do it anyway."

"No."

"No?"

"In this case, I made you do it because a little oral never hurt anyone. But you can always say no if you have misgivings. I'll consider your thoughts, at least. Okay? But there's a respectful and forthcoming way to discuss your issues and then there's acting like a stubborn baby. Guess what you did tonight?"

"Acted like a stubborn baby?"

"Mm-hm. And I have a feeling, knowing you, it won't be the last time." He took her hands in his and pulled her closer, looking into her eyes, enjoying the tension there. "I'm going to give you a spanking over my knee just to drive the lesson home, because you earned it and I'll never let you wiggle out of anything you've earned. Do you understand?"

"Yes Sir," she whispered, staring down at his cock again. Naughty little miscreant. She probably wasn't listening to a word he said. "Come on. Let's get this over with."

He had to rearrange his swollen shaft to pull her over his lap. She was so sweet, so hesitant. He loved over-the-knee spanking, loved holding a woman's body against his, disciplining her. Kat's curves were delicious, shapely and soft against his thighs.

"Put your hands on the floor, or around my leg if you'd rather. Just keep them out of the way. Or should I hold them?"

"You better hold them. Sir," she added, remembering.

He took her hands in one of his, held them at the small of her back. "Don't fight me. Just relax as much as you can and breathe through the blows when they get hard."

"How hard?"

"Harder than the spanking you got at Masquerade. But not as hard as you probably deserve. And I suppose," he said, stroking her tense ass cheeks, "we should agree on a safeword now, on principle, even though I have no intention of pushing your boundaries. Is there one you particularly like?" He was just wasting time now because it was so fun to look down at her perfectly formed ass.

"I don't know," she said, as he expected. "I can't think of one." *I know, but your ass is fucking beautiful to look at and it's killing me, how you're trembling over my lap.*

"If you ever feel you can't take any more in our future games, say the word 'mercy.' Okay? Loud or soft, and I'll stop. Don't forget."

"Okay. Yes Sir, I won't." She sighed, tensing again. It was all he could do not to fling her down on the bed and have his way with her. Her ass was driving him to the brink of madness.

"And don't use it unless you have to. Don't play games with me, girl, or I'll know."

She looked back over her shoulder at him.

"Sir?"

"Yes, Kat?"

"Could you please get on with it before I piss myself from anxiety?"

Stifling a chuckle, he brought his hand down on her right cheek. She was silent until the fourth or fifth smack when she made a soft pleading sound. He ignored her, warming her up with firm, carefully placed smacks until her entire bottom was uniformly pink. She would bruise less this way, as much as he wanted to mark her. Later. Baby steps. He babied her, his novice subby, but the pleading sounds increased steadily in volume and he had to tighten his grip on her hands when she started to jerk and pull away.

"No. Be still and take it."

"It hurts!"

"Yes, it does. This is a punishment spanking." He stroked her crimson cheeks, letting her rest for just a bit. "I know it hurts, but I'm not trying to turn you on right now. I'm trying to teach you a lesson."

Trying to teach her a lesson but enjoying the show in the meantime. She was kicking, yelping, moaning—and he enjoyed every moment of it. He wanted it to last, and for her part, he could practically hear her getting wetter with every word he spoke. The words were part of the game, the exchange, the turn-on. In fact, the words were the most important part. The mental aspect, the psychological backstory, the verbal exchange, it was the basis of the whole thing. He spanked her squirming, kicking form a little more, until he was afraid she'd either come or cry if he kept going, and then he released her.

She jumped away from him and backed against the wall. Her eyes glistened with unshed tears. He watched her to see what she'd do, what she'd say. She said nothing though, just stood and watched him. He stared at the beating pulse at her neck, her body so vitally beautiful to him. Maybe he saw a little adulation in her eyes warring with shame or fear. Whatever it was, it was gorgeous to look at, so he let her stand there a few moments and compose herself before he reached out his hand.

"Do you want to go home?" he asked her.

She looked at his cock again, still rock-hard, still jutting up against his belly. One-track mind, this one.

"I do have to go home. But maybe not just yet. Sir."

She took the hand he offered. He pulled her back to him, smelled her sugary sensual scent. He pushed her down under him on the bed, turning her onto her stomach so he could see the deep red spank marks on her ass. He caressed the hot globes for long moments, squeezing them with his hands. He felt rich. He felt wistful. *One thousand cranes for a wish.* He reached for a condom and knelt between her legs, spreading her wide. She opened for him without resistance, making a small sound of anticipation. He leaned over her with one hand braced on either side of her head.

"You make me happy," he murmured against the back of her neck. She shivered under him and he felt like shivering too. "You're a good girl and I'm very pleased with you."

She hid her face, biting her fist, unable or unwilling to say anything back. He moved into her slowly, inch by inch. She moaned and arched her hips back against him.

"I know, I know," he whispered. "I know you're turned-on. I'll make you come." She was alive beneath him, reacting to each touch, each stroke without inhibition. Her hands made fists beside her head, grasping at the covers. He pressed those hands into the bed, gripped them in his own and trapping her so she couldn't escape. She came not long after that, rippling jerks and a gasp of wonder, and he came too in waves of deep, explosive pleasure. All of it—tasting her, spanking her, getting to see her walls fall down—it all coalesced into one shimmering peak of ecstasy.

He fell over her, feeling emptied and replete. He lay over her a long time, just nestled inside her, until his cock softened and he had to slip the condom off and pull away. Still she didn't move. He put his ear down on her back and listened to her faint, steady heartbeat. He basked in her lovely scent, the scent he already recognized. He tried to memorize the feel of her skin against his. He breathed her name in her ear, felt her long, soft exhalation.

"Ryan," she whispered.

"Yes, doll?"

"I have to go."

Chapter Six

Kat stayed in her room almost all of Sunday. She didn't want to face her mother. She didn't want to talk to anyone. She needed to be alone. Ryan called and she didn't answer. At dinner she watched the chatter of her large family like a spectator. She felt numb, confused. Detached. Her foray into submission at Ryan's home had sent her world lurching sideways. Pleasure and fear warred with some other new emotion she felt. *Love.*

But that was ridiculous. It all came down to the deep intimacies he demanded and the bodily responses she'd felt. The idea of love was ludicrous and she hated herself for mooning over him. Basically he was just really, really good in bed. She tried to convince herself that's all it was and then tried to forget him altogether. Without success.

After dinner she wandered into her father's small TV room. He was watching a cowboy movie, his favorite. In Westerns the good guys and bad guys were always blatantly obvious. In life, Kat thought...not so much.

"Little princess," he said in Russian as she pulled up a chair beside him. "What's the matter?"

"Nothing."

He grunted. "Something is wrong. You are troubled tonight."

After a moment she sighed. "I just don't know, Papa. I don't know."

"Don't know what, *zaika*?"

"I don't know how to change. I don't know how to stop doing things that...that make me...unhappy..." Her throat closed on the last word, making a pathetic strangling sound that very much expressed how she felt. Her papa reached for her hand, clasped it tightly.

"You must not be unhappy. This is not good."

"I know."

They both fell silent, sat together in comfortable stillness. Her papa always soothed her when no one else could, because he would just hold her hand and make no other demands on her. She looked down at his hand in hers, parchment white, with more liver spots than she remembered. Her papa was getting old. She was getting old. Life was rolling along, rolling past her with a velocity she didn't know how to halt.

"How did you know, when you met Mama?" she asked. "How did you know she was the one for you? Did you love her right away?"

He blinked, looking past her, considering. "Ah, Katyusha," he murmured. "I don't remember."

"I'm sorry."

"But you know what?" he said a moment later. "It does not matter how or when you know. It matters that you love, not how you know or how you find it. If you love, you love." He looked back at his cowboy movie, waved his other hand in a light gesture. "Katya, you think too much. You have too much intelligence. This is my fault, I fear."

Kat laughed softly. "Yes. It's all your fault."

He squeezed her hand, warm gentle pressure. "Are you... Are you in love?"

"No. I don't think so. I don't know."

"Don't know? *Poufft.*" He tore his gaze from the flickering Western to look over at her hard and took her chin in his hand. "It is very important to know. And yet not important at all. Do you understand what I mean?"

"Nope. Not at all."

Fortune

"Ah well. You know...love...it begins in the heart, not up here," he said, tapping her temple. "It is not thinking and knowing, *zaika*. It is feeling. How do you feel? Mama tells me it is the doctor you are seeing. This is true?"

"Yes. I suppose."

"And how do you feel about him?"

"I don't know. That's just it. I don't know how I feel about him."

"Knowing is nothing. How do you feel? Here?" He laid a hand on her heart. She looked at him, considering.

"I feel scared," she finally said. "I feel anxious."

"Oh." Her father's brows drew together and he turned back to his show. "In that case..."

She waited a moment. "In that case, what, Papa?"

He stared back at her, a million miles away. She kissed him on his cheek and squeezed his hand. She watched the rest of the Western with him in silence until his grip loosened on her hand and he drifted to sleep. When Kat left to go up to her room and get ready to go out, her mama watched her closely but, for once, held her tongue.

* * * * *

The gay club was the place to be Sunday night. For years she'd come here to soak in the fun. The place was cavernous, dark, smoky, a thousand times cooler than Masquerade. The music was louder and more current, and the man flesh was definitely hotter, albeit not interested in her. Still, it was a great place to lose herself. At least it used to be.

Kat felt more and more like an outsider at the clubs. Since she'd taken a few weeks off, since her tumble down the stairs, since *him*...the clubs didn't feel the same. She felt trapped between her past life and her future—a future she didn't know yet. She felt alone, stranded. No one talked to her. She realized there was only one person who wanted to talk to her and that was the person whose calls she'd ignored all day. She left her phone at home, thinking to escape him, thinking to come out to the clubs and have a blast the way she always had. Thinking to prove to herself that she didn't need him at all.

To her chagrin, she found she had never wanted him more.

She made her way through the throngs of hard, sweaty bodies and pounding drumbeats to the fresh coolness outside. She headed to a pay phone only to realize she had no change. She sweet-talked a lesbian in line out of some change and returned to the phone only to remember she didn't know his number. She thought just a moment before she turned and began to walk. So convenient, that he lived in Cambridge. Cambridge was close, a few blocks walk. She knew his street and was fairly sure she would remember his house. She looked at her watch. It was nearly one. She hoped she remembered his house or she might really alarm somebody.

When she got to the door she thought was his, she knocked softly. If this wasn't his house, she hoped no one answered with a gun. After another moment, she screwed up her courage and rang the bell. She had to be crazy. What was she doing here? She took a deep breath, a couple seconds away from aborting her mission, when the lock turned. The door swung open and he stood looking out at her through the storm door, rubbing his tousled hair. He was shirtless, in jersey gympants that rode low on his hips, drawing her eyes there. She quickly looked back up at his face, blushing.

He opened the door to let her into the foyer. "Kat. Are you okay? What are you doing here?"

It suddenly occurred to her that he had most certainly been sleeping. He probably had work early in the morning. God, he was probably going to screw up and kill someone on the operating table, all because she'd decided she had to see him tonight.

"I'm sorry I woke you."

"I wasn't sleeping. Answer my question. What are you doing here?" He looked over her shoulder, outside. "Did you walk?"

"I walked from Club Bronze. It wasn't far."

He made a face, a quiet sound of frustration. "And now here you are. It's one in the morning. I called you several times today to see if you wanted to come over."

"I...I didn't answer."

"I know."

"I'm sorry. You have to understand...understand—"

"You need to understand this, Ekaterina," he said, cutting her off in a curt, impatient voice. "If I let you in here, you're not just going to take what you want and skip on home."

"Take what I want? I don't... I don't even know what you're talking about."

His jaw tightened. He reached behind her and opened the storm door. "Out."

"Please..." She bit her lip, at a loss for words. She needed him, needed his help, but he was too annoyed to give it to her. She looked up at him in the semidarkness, at his nearly black eyes, his pursed, impatient lips. She felt guilty, desperate to mollify his irritated mood. "Please let me stay, Ryan. Please...I...I need you."

"Why?" he asked sharply. "Why do you need me?"

"Because. Because..." She knew she had to come up with something plausible, something believable. "Because..." She put her hand over her heart, thought of her papa. "Because I feel something here. And it really hurts. Can you help me? You're a doctor."

His expression softened. He might have even chuckled softly under his breath. "Cardiac is not my field, Kat." He put his hand on her waist, just a tentative brush of fingertips, but it held her immobile. He gazed at her, hard intention and seriousness again. "If I let you in, you're spending the night with me. You're sleeping in my bed until morning."

"I'll spend the whole week. I'll spend the whole month in your bed if you want. Just please—"

Her voice cut off on a quaver as his arms came around her. He bent his head to her, nuzzled her neck, ran insistent fingers into her hair and tugged a little, tilting her head back. His lips settled over hers and she went loose and shivery in his arms. All the loneliness and confusion, all the numbness went away. He was warm and solid, clasping her close. He smelled fresh and clean, just-showered, not smoky and brittle like her. "I'm sorry," she said, and "I missed you." She breathed the words against his lips when he let her come up for air. He didn't reply, only kissed her again, pressing against her so she felt the solid outline of his cock against her front.

"It's late," she whispered then.

"Never too late," he whispered back, leading her toward his room.

She felt a strange peace, a warm fuzziness as he pulled her down the hall behind him. She felt it in her chest and in her pelvis. She loved the way his hand clasped hers so tightly. She gazed up at his broad back and straight shoulders as she followed him, stared at the movement of his hips. A faint light issued from his room and again she felt guilt that she had awakened him.

But as she slipped behind him into the bedroom, she saw he hadn't been sleeping at all. His bed was covered in a mess of glossy multicolored paper squares and already folded cranes. There were piles of them, perhaps a hundred or more. He looked sheepish for a moment, the corner of his lip drawn up in a self-deprecating smile. "I make them sometimes when I'm anxious. Frustrated." He moved to the bed and swept them to the floor in a careless movement that startled her.

"Oh, Ryan. They'll break. They'll get crushed down there."

He spun to her. His dark eyes blinked, once, twice. "They're only paper. Isn't that what you said once? You're more important right now. Come here."

She went to him, feeling mournful about the swiped-away, scattered figures. "What are you so anxious about?" She thought of the stressful work he did, complicated surgeries and consultations.

"You," he growled. He kissed her again, harder, deeper, his fingers fumbling with the zipper at the back of her dress. She sensed anger in his touch and wondered why it didn't scare her. Perhaps it wasn't anger, only need. She knew she needed him. She helped him pull off her tights with trembling fingers, let him unhook her bra and toss it behind her. She had on skimpy panties—she heard the seam rip as he shoved his hand down the waistband and grabbed her ass, cupping and squeezing it with rough urgency. It was still sore from... Was it just last night he'd spanked her? With a soft grunt, he tore off the filmy panties, tossing them somewhere over by her bra. He slapped her ass hard and she cried out, more from arousal than the sting. He slapped her again and she pressed closer to him, grasped at him, whining into the hollow of his neck. He nudged her head back and kissed her with voracious, focused intent even as he slapped her ass a third time. She moaned into his mouth as dull throbbing heat spread across her ass cheeks and down to the center between her legs. She wanted to cry out *Fuck me! Take me!* But she knew instinctively that he would not appreciate orders from her, especially not in his current mood.

He drew away from her with another low sound of pent-up frustration. "Go. Go lie on the bed. On your back. Arms over your head."

His words barely registered and yet her body moved to do just as he asked. No, not asked. *Required.* He kicked off his sweatpants and looked back at her watching him. She was afraid of what he might do to her, but she couldn't have left for anything. He opened a drawer and rooted around in the low light, producing a pair of thick leather cuffs. He strode back to the bed and she stared at the sight of him. He was all force and strength, his abs contracting, his arms poised at his side, arms Kat believed could hold up the earth if they had to. He crawled onto the bed, knelt beside her and pulled her hands up hard above her so she felt manhandled. He buckled the cuffs on with a quickness and ease born of experience and hooked them behind one of the spindles on the headboard of his bed.

"Oh," she sighed.

He looked down at her. "Oh, what? Too tight? Do they feel okay?"

"I think I'm going to die." Silly words. But honestly, how else to describe it? Her pussy felt alive with need, aching for him. Her whole body pulsed. She pulled at the restraints as he watched her, then turned her hips to one side in a defensive—or perhaps desperate—movement. He reached down, his eyes black in the soft light, and thrust two fingers roughly up inside her. She was so wet, so wet. What must he think? He smiled down at her, a knowing grin.

"I've half a mind to leave you this way. This is fun to watch. And I think you deserve it."

Her breath caught in her throat. He couldn't be so cruel. "Please!"

"You and your never-ending 'pleases'. All they mean is give me what I want."

"No. I mean, yes. I want you. But please... Sir...what do you want? I'll give you anything."

He laughed and knelt over her, straddling her. He brought his fingers to her mouth, soaked with her feminine essence. "Anything? Suck," he said softly. "Suck my fingers clean, then suck my cock."

She tasted herself, her own arousal and need on his broad fingers. He leaned forward and guided his cock to her mouth, leaning over her so she was trapped, impaled. He felt so thick, so hard between her lips. She licked around the velvety tip, exploring the rigid contours. When he moved deeper into her, her mouth was wet and ready. She realized she had salivated for him, eager to take his length.

"Open your eyes."

She looked up, opened her eyes and peered up at the man who subdued her, who was staring down at her while he eased his cock in and out of her mouth. He looked feral for a moment. Terrifying. Her hands moved in the rough cuffs, made fists and twisted in a small panic. Then he whispered, "Good girl."

He withdrew from her slowly. Her mouth still waited, open, feeling empty. He leaned down and kissed her hard, his tongue now pressing into her mouth. He licked her lips, groaned softly against her as her hips rose up to contact his cock wedged between them. With a stifled curse he tore himself away and lunged for the bedside drawer. He ripped open the condom and rolled on the latex barrier, then shoved her legs apart, wide, wider, until she squeaked. He slapped her between the legs, on the inside of each thigh. It was pain, but desperate, abject pleasure. She needed to be filled by him. The emptiness inside her was at its peak. The sensation, the slaps, the pinches, the strokes had built to an unbearable, insupportable tension.

"Please," she whispered. *Please, a million times.*

He pulled her knees up, spreading her wider, pulling her down against her bonds. He sat back on his heels so his cock jutted up between them, nestled at her entrance. He looked down at her then, a predator going for the kill. She wanted to look away it was so frightening, but she didn't dare. He dropped his hips and squeezed her thighs and thrust inside her, his size a pressing, invading ache. She burst into tears, not from pain or fear, but relief. She was going to come in seconds, mere moments. She looked up at him, frantic, and he nodded down at her. "Go," he said. "Go on. I've got you."

She came apart. She shattered, she shimmered. She convulsed and lost herself in an orgasm that turned her upside down. He just watched her with a faint victorious smile, amused affection. Then he fell over her, pumped in her hard so her cuffs rattled against the headboard. His knees drove into the bed between her legs. The rough hair on his chest chafed her and his hands gripped her arms, holding her down, down, down, hard and fast. He overpowered her completely. When he came, shuddering, he crushed her so she could barely breathe. She lay still beneath him, feeling peace at last.

He was still a little in shock. When she hadn't answered his calls, he'd tried to write her off, cut her out of his heart. Part of him thought that was the better thing to do. But then seeing her there at the door, hearing her plead with him to let her stay... His resolve crumbled, vanquished by her lush needful body. Now he held her close, tucking her head in the crook of his shoulder. Her soft dark curls tickled his chest and her skin was impossibly velvety and soft against his. He ran his fingertips over her, from perfectly formed breasts to delicate waist and hips, to smooth thighs.

They started to talk after a while, quiet negotiating. What they discussed was important but his mind was elsewhere. Between her legs. Wrapped around her fingers. Sliding over her hips.

"The thing is," she said in a soft voice, "I won't always want to call you Sir."

He looked back at her, trying to concentrate over the sensory shock of having her so near, so sweet and pliable next to him. He ran a finger down her jaw, stroked her chin. He kissed her softly and framed a tentative answer. "Of course you won't."

"But I don't know if...if you only like me as a submissive."

"I like you as Kat. What about you? Do you only like me as a Dominant?"

"No. That's only part of it." She drew her fingertips through the hair on his chest, a casual gesture that made his jaw tense. Her caresses were a rousing pleasure he felt in his balls and his cock. He leaned down to kiss her again, a messy wet kiss, his groin tightening—his constant response to her. He fed on her rare sweetness and openness. When they drew apart he rested his hand on one of her lovely ass cheeks and looked down at her thoughtfully.

"Did you mean what you said about sleeping here for a month?"

She looked taken aback. Her eyes blinked once, twice. "I could... I... Are you... Would you want me to?"

"Yes."

She coughed softly, her fingertips stopping on his chest to curl into a fist. He expected her to push away from him but she didn't. "Why would you want that?" she asked.

He chuckled. "Don't you?" His hand roved down the satin curve of her hip to the juncture of her thighs, to the slick treasure there. She tensed and buried her head in his neck as he teased her clit. Her hips pressed closer to him and his cock throbbed in reaction, jabbing against her. He reached for a condom. She didn't protest, didn't draw away as he sheathed himself and moved over her. He entered her in a slow, liquid movement, holding her still with a hand on each hip. The pleasure was thick and heavy along his shaft, like a lazy humid afternoon when you didn't want to move. He stayed still in her, feeling her closeness, smelling her female scent. She moved her hips, just a twitch, but he shook his head and tsked at her.

"Be still a minute, doll. I'm not done talking with you."

She looked up at him, her eyes hazy with pleasure now. "I'm finding it harder to concentrate," she whispered. He pinched her nipple hard, then harder. The haziness in her eyes dissipated. She jerked as the pain registered and still he pinched her harder until she sobbed, soft and quick. She put her hand on his but he didn't let go. "This is why you want me here. Sex," she said with mild accusation. "You want to fuck me whenever you want."

He released her nipple abruptly. "No. That's not why. There are so many more reasons." He pulled out of her. She pressed against him with a small whine but he held himself away. "Stay with me for a month. Just a month."

"My mother won't like it."

"Your mother will pack your bags for you and you know it."

Her mouth twisted into a wry smile. "Yeah. She really likes you."

"Because she knows I would be good for you."

He could tell Kat was thinking it over. He stayed still, not wanting to hear a *no* or anything negative. He stayed still, willing what he wanted to happen. He glanced past her, just for a fleeting moment, at all the cranes on the floor.

"I don't want to be your submissive all the time," she said. "I don't want to be with you all the time. So I just don't know."

"I won't be here a lot of the time. I'll be at work."

"I work too."

"I know. I understand you'll need your own time. I will too."

"I want my own room."

"No."

"Yes."

"Maybe." He nudged his cock against her center, just enough to make her sigh. "If you're a good girl."

She melted as she always did when he talked about good girls. Not that she was one, not even close. Not that he wanted her to be. He pinched her nipple again, thrust his tongue into her mouth to taste her.

"Oh, Ryan," she sighed when he drew away from her. "Okay. I guess I will."

He held himself over her, going still. "You will?"

"Why not?"

Why not? It wasn't exactly unbridled enthusiasm, but it was enough. "Yes, Kat. Why not?" he said, gathering her closer with a hard breath. He sank into her, pounded into her, not being gentle. He spilled all his hopes and fantasies into her questing hips, her gripping thighs. He groped at her breasts, squeezed them until she groaned and tried to twist away. He kissed her until she was breathless. He cast his fortune at her feet. Later he would pick up the cranes, string them into groups of forty until he had one thousand. *Senbazuru.*

"I know you'll be sorry," she said in his ear. "I know I'll drive you crazy."

"I know it too," he said. "I know."

* * * * *

They finally slept. He could have fucked her until dawn but he had a surgery scheduled, so he left her alone after he extracted her promise to move in. One month. He wanted more, but he would take a month for the present. In a month he would know if they were compatible or not, and she would too. He watched her fall asleep in his arms, at peace now that the decision had been made, now that she'd finally capitulated. But he felt less peace now and more pressure. She'd torn down her walls, at least a little, for him. Now he had to prevent her from building them up again.

But it was an improvement on before. Before she showed up, he'd spent a couple hours folding cranes, wishing for…what? To forget her? To possess her? To find what he sought? His fingers made the figures by memory now, thoughtless folds and creases, a tip down of head and beak.

When he'd realized the sheer number of cranes he'd folded, when Kat saw them all, it embarrassed him a bit. God knew what she thought.

The next morning he woke before her, completely unwilling to get out of bed and leave her there, but not wanting to wake her prematurely. She looked so content, so peaceful in sleep. He drowsed beside her as long as he could, until his erection was too intense to ignore. He pressed it against her backside, bold now that he'd decided to take action. She stirred, squirming back against him, stretching like a cat.

"Ekaterina," he murmured into her neck. "I have something for you. A big present."

She laughed, looking over her shoulder at him. He stared, beguiled, at her too-fleeting smile. Someday she would smile all the time for him, smile and laugh out loud until her cheekbones ached. Goals. Life was nothing without goals. His present goal, however, was impaling her with his cock, which he'd already half accomplished. He fumbled in the bedside table for a condom, thinking to himself that he'd drag her in for blood tests that very week. He wanted to sink inside her without any barrier between them. He wanted every barrier breached, consigned to history. He reached around her to bury his fingers in her folds, to find her clit. She was already receptive and wet.

He fucked her from behind, holding her close and tight against him. "Now listen to me," he growled against her ear as he slid in and out of her. "After work today, you go home and get ready to come stay. Pack your stuff. Tell your parents what's going on, however you want to explain it. I'll swing by to get you later. Understand?" He gripped her pussy in his hand, pushed hard into her from behind.

"Yes," she said.

"Yes Sir. I understand."

Fortune

"Yes Sir, I understand," she repeated in a sweet sober voice, pressing her head back under his chin. Absolutely everything had changed. She was almost unrecognizable from the girl she was just a few nights ago. She was more open to him and so much less afraid. Miraculous. He drove into her, feeling her cool skin slide over his. Each time he entered her she gave a delighted sigh. Her hand crept back and clung to his leg, dug in with a spasmodic grip. It was a small discomfort to balance the hot overwhelming pleasure. Her moans crested and her fingers bruised him. He took her hand hard in his, stroking her clit with the other hand until he felt the release, the gasping, the contraction of her walls around his cock. He grabbed her then, bucked against her as his own orgasm unfurled and shook him. He was rocked by the intensity of his feelings for her, by the draw that grew stronger the closer she got. He thought, with the one small part of his brain that still functioned, that he needed to proceed carefully. Perhaps she was right about having time alone, about keeping separate rooms. He thought perhaps they needed to keep some distance between them until their relationship as Dom and sub was developed and set.

He told her so as they sat bleary-eyed over a quick breakfast of toast and grapefruit. "Maybe we can set up times when we're 'on' and times when we're 'off'. Certain nights and times," he said.

"Okay." She shrugged her shoulders a bit.

"Would you care for some soy milk with your toast?"

She looked up at him in consternation. "I'm afraid soy milk is a hard limit for me."

"It's a lot healthier than cow's milk."

"Um, no thank you. I'm not really that into grapefruit either."

"You need at least eight to nine servings of fruits and vegetables a day."

"Don't you mean eight to nine servings a month? 'Cause that's what I normally average."

He thumped her lightly on the head. "At least eat the toast."

"Little controlling, aren't you?"

"Sometimes. But you're a little out of control. Aren't you?"

She looked down, blushing slightly. "Sometimes."

"Anyway, I think we could make things work between us. You wouldn't always need to be under my control. You could have time to yourself and we could still hang out. Get to know each other as people and not just D/s roles. I think it would be good. Healthy. Everything in balance."

"I think so too. I don't want to lose sight of real life in…all this."

All this. As she said that, she gestured vaguely with one small hand, waving away what was between them with those two words. Or maybe casting a spell, like an incantation. *All this magic between us… Let's not lose sight of real life.*

He didn't know her well enough yet to interpret what she meant by that little hand wave, but he was determined to learn.

Chapter Seven

"Dr. McCarthy?"

Ryan turned to see one of the neuro nurses poking her head in the door. "Yes, Kelly?"

"Did you want to sign off on Mr. Bellman's papers?"

"I don't believe I need to."

"Oh." She feigned confusion, double-checked the papers. Ryan was already turning around, trying to refocus on his work. Kelly was one of a handful of nurses who liked to trump up reasons to interrupt him, to come into his office when he was at the hospital and wave around her fake nails and boobs. Wild, bombshell blondes had attracted him at one point, admittedly.

But not now. Now he only wanted shiny dark curls and light green eyes.

Kelly paused, perhaps considering another tack, but to his relief he heard the door close. He was eager to finish up and get his notes in order for tomorrow. He had a feeling he'd be preoccupied at home tonight.

At home. Home took on a whole new meaning, knowing she would be there now. Home, for him, had always meant quiet. Structure. Solitude. He'd never lived with a woman, never wanted to. He went out to the clubs and bars when he wanted sex, when he wanted to party, and came home later alone. It wasn't that he didn't want a lively homelife someday—he just wanted it on his terms. To tell the truth, he'd always harbored vague, distant fantasies of a vibrant home front, a doting wife, wonderful kids, holidays and parties and togetherness. Something like Kat's family, a loving, intertwined unit that stuck together. Constant activity, companionship and a shoulder to lean on. Blood was thicker than water. He was a doctor. He knew.

He finished checking off his notes and appointments then closed his laptop. He left some paperwork for Kelly to deal with and moved resolutely to the door, noting it was 6:05. He'd been aiming for 6:00 but he would take it. It wasn't far to Kat's house. On the way to the car, his phone buzzed. He thought it might be Kat but she was pretty phone-avoidant. He looked down to see his friend Dave's number instead.

"Dave!"

"You in surgery, man?"

Ryan laughed. "If I was I wouldn't be answering. We've been over this before. How are you? How are Sophie and Hunter?"

"They're great. The little guy's growing like a weed. Sophie wants me to make him stop but I don't know how."

"Typical subby. Thinks you have the answer to everything."

"Well, I usually do," chuckled Dave. "I've trained her well. What about you? How are things with your new girl?"

Ryan drew in a deep breath. "I'm going to see her now. Get this. She's moving in."

There was a short silence on the other line. "Er... Who are you? And how did you get my friend's phone? 'Cause the Ryan I know doesn't live with girls."

"I know. I think I may live to regret it."

"Or she may," snickered Dave. "She must be a glutton for punishment."

"She's a glutton for punishment *and* sex. So I can't complain. We'll work the rest out." He sobered, clearing his throat. "But really. I don't know. I hope it does work out."

Dave was silent a moment, picking up on Ryan's pensive vibe. They had always been that way, childhood friends, able to tell each other's moods from nothing more than the tone in their voice. "So who is this girl who's tamed the beast? She's special, huh?"

"Yeah," said Ryan. "She's...different. I can't explain. When you met Sophie...you told me once that you knew right away. The first day you met her. The first time you talked."

"Sure. I guess it was that way. At the time it just felt like infatuation. Or madness. But looking back, that's what it was. We just matched. I don't know how else to explain it."

"I get that feeling too with this girl. Problem is, I'm not so sure the feeling is mutual."

"Well, she's moving in. That's a pretty big commitment."

"She's moving in for a month."

"A month? Like...just a month?"

"The jury's still out on that."

"Oh, okay. I see. Well, work your magic. Dom her into submission. You've always done that in the past."

"I know. It's just that now..." His voice trailed off.

"The stakes are higher."

"Yeah." Ryan laughed softly. "See. You always know."

"I have been there, done that, my friend. Either way you'll come out on the other side, right? So don't stress. And look, if things work out, I'll be happy to take your wedding pictures."

Ryan groaned, turning into Kat's street. "One step at a time. A month from now I might be calling to tell you she's driving me nuts."

"Come on. Think positive. Hey, I'll be up in your neck of the woods for a photog convention in February. Maybe me and Soph can meet this new little sub of yours. That would be fun, huh?"

Ryan smiled as he parked and turned off the engine. "Down, boy. She's been practically vanilla up to this point. I don't know how she'd take to a ménage a couple months in."

"Vanilla?" Dave scoffed. "If you've been with her, she's halfway to chocolate by now. Rocky Road. Moose Tracks."

"Okay, okay," Ryan laughed. "I've got to go."

Ryan tucked the phone back in his pocket. He pulled at his tie while looking in the rearview mirror, attempting to straighten it. He thought he should have changed his clothes before he came over, but then perhaps his office dress would impress Kat's parents more. One should look their best when showing up to take someone's daughter home to move in. He rang the bell, thinking for the first time what he might do if her mother forbade it. As if on cue, the door swung open and Elena stood with a dubious look on her face.

"Dr. Ryan." Elena peered out at him as she stood on the doorstep, her greeting typically loud and blunt.

"Is Kat here?" he asked.

"She is here," answered Elena, threading her arm under his and pulling him in. "But I think before you go, you come to dinner. We discuss a few things. We talk."

* * * * *

Kat had to bite her lip not to laugh at the look on his face.

She could see he was trying his very best to present himself as the responsible and well-intentioned suitor. To be honest he was doing quite well, but Kat recognized the nervous tension underneath.

Sure, she could have called and warned him that Elena would make him stay for dinner, make him undergo an interrogation only slightly less aggressive than those conducted by the State Department. She could have, but that would have ruined all the fun. Anyway, he should have known. When he was just a "friend", a successful doctor and polite dinner guest who seemed to have a passing interest in her daughter, that was one thing. Now he was something else... A prospective son-in-law.

At least her mother jumped to that conclusion. Kat had told her nothing of the "one month" agreement or her dabbles in power exchange with the fresh-faced young doctor in the spiffy tie. In Kat's family, when you moved in with someone it was to practice for marriage. Kat hadn't told Ryan that, hadn't seen a need. But he realized it now, certainly. Elena had just pried the last few generations of his ancestry from him in conversation. Now she was moving on to religious and political beliefs. Next would be questions designed to intuit his morality, his integrity on personal issues Elena considered important. Fidelity, personal responsibility, social issues. She'd heard it all before, witnessed this dissection with each of her sisters' husbands.

She only half listened, tuning in for the parts where he revealed something that surprised her. Stepsiblings she didn't know he had, a childhood sojourn in the Far East. Agnostic beliefs that were well thought out and interesting. But she already knew most of what she needed to know about him. Everything else was extraneous, insights she wasn't in the mood to analyze. Some part of her didn't want to know him that well. Some part of her wanted to preserve a distance. She knew he could control her—he'd proven that already. She wasn't quite ready yet to give up that control. She thought he could get a dangerous grip on her if he wanted to.

She fully intended to move out at the end of a month. She knew she'd be over him by then, probably long before then actually. She was always that way... Got obsessed with something or someone and moved on when she'd scratched the itch. She'd done her best to warn him that she wasn't good relationship material, so she wasn't going to waste a lot of time feeling guilty when she left. Or feeling guilty while she watched him squirm through Elena's questions.

"And you want children, I guess?" Elena asked him with a smile.

"Oh yes, Mrs. Argounov. Tons of them."

Kat choked on piece of dinner roll. Her father's face lit up over his cabbage and potatoes. Ryan looked around the table at Kat's sisters, at their messy, squalling babies and impish children.

"You know, I think that's the real meaning of life. Love, connection, family. All this. You all... You don't know how lucky you are. Or perhaps you do."

Kat almost applauded. What a slam dunk. Her mother would be pure putty in his hands now. Elena looked around at her family too, the beaming matriarch. "I share your idea, Dr. Ryan. I like this idea of family."

"Please, call me Ryan," he said, reaching for Kat beside him. He put his arm around her, pulled her close and kissed her forehead. Kat looked past him to see her father's eyes shining, a tremulous smile on his face.

* * * * *

"That was really wrong of you," she told him on the way to his house after dinner.

"What was really wrong?"

"Leading them on like that. Feeding them those bullshit lines about kids and family. I can't believe my mother at least, couldn't see through you."

He glanced over at her, then back at the road. "It's not bullshit. I didn't tell one lie to your mother or father. I told you, Kat. I never lie."

"Well," she said, feeling sulky at the reprimand in his tone. "You were trying to manipulate them. You manipulate people. I've seen you do it. You manipulate me." He made a soft sound, a cross between a laugh and a sigh. "Do you deny it?"

"I manipulate you every chance I get, doll."

"Ugh. Why do you keep calling me that?"

"Because I want to. Get used to it, doll. And you're no stranger to manipulation, if you're going to be pointing fingers."

She fell silent, watching the tree-lined sidewalks out the window, the tiny Cambridge house gardens. Little disciplined managed plots of color maintained in a crowded Boston suburb. She thought she would be disciplined and maintained that way by Ryan. He would try to make her thrive where she didn't naturally belong. And her mother and father were one hundred percent behind him — as Ryan had forecast, Elena practically packed her bags and carried them out to Ryan's car. She felt anxious, scared. Excited. Ryan looked over at her and stroked her thigh softly for just a moment.

"You're going to spend tonight without any clothes. When we get home, they come off and you stay naked until tomorrow morning when you go to work. Understood?"

"Um…"

"Yes Sir."

"Yes Sir. But um…may I ask a question?"

"Sure."

"Is that every night? Or just tonight?"

"It's whenever I say so."

Kat looked down in her lap, at her hands clasped there. "Oh. What if I get cold?"

"You won't get cold."

The way he said it left no mystery behind the meaning. When they got to his house, he took her inside and had her strip in the foyer. He took her clothes down the hall, into the room that was "hers". He returned and approached her in silence with that intent look that always rattled her a little, made her want to hide herself. He put his hands on her, pressing on the small of her back so she had to stand up straighter. He pushed back her shoulders so her breasts were thrust forward.

"Don't slouch. Stand up straight and present yourself to me."

"For...for what?"

"For my pleasure." His curt words made some wild drumbeat commence between her legs. Her stomach flipped over and fluttered, although she tried to remain outwardly cool. Inside she was anything but. Her pussy was already growing wet and ready for him. He pulled at her arms. "Let them fall naturally at your side. Stand straight and open to me." *Breathe in, breathe out.* He put his thumb under her chin, tipped her head up and straight. He looked into her eyes with that dark gaze that burned and searched her expression. She stared back, knowing it was expected. What did he see? Why did she imagine he saw more than she even knew of herself? He put his hands on her neck and rested them there, not moving her or controlling her. She straightened unconsciously, then licked her lips.

"Are you going to put a collar on me?" she asked, trying to sound flippant.

"Not yet." His voice didn't sound flippant at all. "Someday. When I think you're up for it." He chucked her under the chin. "Baby steps. Now..." He stepped back and scrutinized her, tipped her shoulders back just one more iota. The positioning felt unnatural but he seemed to want that. "I'm going to bring your things in and put them in your room. You're going to stand there and you're not going to move. Not one inch. When I'm done bringing your things in, I'm going to take you in the bedroom and hurt you. Then I'm going to fuck you and put you to bed for the night. Any questions?"

She had trouble finding her voice. "No," she finally managed. He gave her a dire look. "No Sir," she corrected quickly.

With one last sweeping inspection of her body, he turned and went out the door. Kat found herself alone with her thoughts, standing naked and still at the behest of her Master. She was acutely aware of the heaviness of her breasts, the rise and fall of her chest, the vulnerability of her bared ass cheeks as the cool air blew across them. The mounting heat at the apex of her thighs.

He made several trips, pausing each time to inspect her on entering. Her face burned from the scrutiny. The third time, before he headed back to the car, he took her wrists and pulled her hands up. "Lace your fingers at the back of your neck. Elbows out. Stand up straight." She swallowed and did as he asked. He wasn't happy with her efforts. He pushed her elbows back until her breasts were forced even farther forward. Then, silently, he went around behind her and drove his knee between her legs. He began to spread them open, using his leather shoes to push her bare feet a distance apart on the floor.

She was strangled with lust and yet terrified. Cool air rushed up into her exposed center. She was terrified he would touch her and yet terrified he wouldn't. He didn't touch her, though, or say another word, just gave her another fathomless stare and turned away to make another trip to the car.

It felt like hours that she stood there, but the clock said ten minutes. He brought the last of her things in and then returned to take her arm, pulling her from her rigid stance. "You can unpack tomorrow."

He didn't wait for any answer to that and she didn't attempt one. In his bedroom he arranged her again. She was already quicker at it. Shoulders back, hips straight, ankles together, arms at her side. He gave a small nod, acknowledging her progress, however minor. When she was positioned to his liking he turned away and undressed, taking his time. He took off his tie, hung it on the tie rack. Undid his belt, hung it on another rack. Folded his pants and shirt and put them in a pile for the dry cleaners. She watched his muscles as he worked, as he leaned and reached and strode to the closet. So much leashed power. It seemed inconceivable that this man spent his days performing neurosurgery, dealing in fine increments too small to be detected by the human eye.

So much steadiness, so much finesse must have been required, and yet there was a wildness in him she could barely comprehend.

When he was fully undressed, he crossed in front of her to his bureau and pulled open the bottom drawer. It was filled with neatly coiled and tied-off bunches of rope of several thicknesses and colors. She watched as he sorted through them thoughtfully.

"Are you planning to hang me?"

He turned. "That would kind of defeat the purpose." He looked back in the drawer, drew out some rope, twisted it between his fingers as if testing the weight and softness. He stood and came to her, unraveling the bundle. "Kat, have you ever heard of shibari?"

"Is that some kind of power drink?" He took one nipple between thumb and forefinger, pinching a sharp warning. "Uh...um...some kinky rope thing?" she guessed again.

"Shibari is another word for Japanese rope bondage. And it's not just kinky stuff. It's an art form." He gestured back toward the drawer. "As you may have guessed from my collection, I'm pretty into it." He lifted the frayed edge of the rope he held, drew it across the tender nipple he'd just pinched. She shivered at the ticklish sensation. "I'm going to tie you up, Kat."

"Um, okay. For how long?"

"For as long as I want."

"Somehow I knew you were going to say that."

"Hush, you little brat." He made her kneel, then pressed her forward until her forehead touched the carpet. "Give me your hands." She reached them back and he took them, cinching them together wrist-to-wrist with the rope. He ran the dangling tails around her waist and crossed them at the front, then pulled them back up again.

As he worked, she rested her cheek on the floor and gazed over at the jumble of paper cranes still scattered on the floor. She thought she should pick them up. At least someone should. All that careful, intricate work. Behind her back, the same fingers that had folded the cranes whispered across her skin, punctuated sometimes by the touch of soft, scratchy rope. He got up at one point and moved back across the room. She heard a drawer opening and closing but she couldn't turn her head up high enough to see what he returned with. He put whatever it was on the small desk against the wall and knelt down again. She was still, compliant. She was curious about what the hell was going on. She felt the rope almost like a blanket on her back, a crisscrossing pattern. She felt a little tug and then rope being tied around her ankles.

That finished, he stood a couple paces in front of her and said, "Come here."

She started to move, rousing the usual muscles into action. She thought the rope behind her was loose enough to allow motion, but her legs stopped still. Her torso lurched, arrested. He caught her shoulders before she did a faceplant into the rug. "Jesus," she snapped. "What the fuck?"

"Try again. Slowly. Come here. Think about how you'll have to move."

Kat felt sudden tears burn behind her eyes. She felt humiliated, helpless. "I can't move at all. You tied me up."

"I've hampered you, but you can still move."

"I don't want to do this anymore." She hunkered over, resting her head on the floor. She hated the tremor in her voice.

He squatted down in front of her, patted the side of her hair as if she were a child or a pet. She wanted to pull away but she couldn't. "Don't be a quitter, Kat. And don't overreact right now. How are you feeling?"

She pulled at the bonds, at her arms and legs hobbled and no longer under her control. "I feel restricted. Trapped."

"Good. That's how I meant you to feel." He kept petting her, stroking her hair. "You're trapped but I've got you. You're okay. Do you understand? Now try it again." He stood in front of her again, a towering pillar to her supplication. "Move. Come here."

She moved more slowly, more carefully this time. He made an encouraging sound. She discovered that if she inched each knee forward and distributed her weight carefully, she could move forward without falling or tipping on her side. As she moved forward, he moved back. With painstaking progress she inched across his bedroom.

"Good girl," he said finally. "Stop. Remind me what I said I was going to do to you here in the bedroom."

"I was kind of hoping you were going to fuck me, but I'm not sure how you'd accomplish that with this—owww!" A slice of liquid fire lanced across her buttocks, and then another. *Owww.* It took a moment for it to register that *he* was doing it. There was a disconnect before she understood that he had brought back some implement from those drawers and was using it on her now. It took another moment for her to understand that she also had no power to get away, to evade any further blows. By the third stroke, the throbbing scary pain had her scrambling for an answer, any answer to make it stop. "Oww! Umm...ahh..."

"What did I say? Weren't you listening?"

God, she needed to listen better. She thought back, thought hard. *When I'm done bringing your things in, I'm going to take you in the bedroom and hurt you.* "You—you said you were going to hurt me."

"Very good."

"Which you're kind of doing right now—ouch!" She gasped and tensed at the sudden stinging pain, cursing her sassy mouth. She clamped her lips shut, drawing her legs in more tightly.

"Finished?"

"Yes Sir." She heard him put the implement back down on the desk, a minute sound that still registered in the form of relief. He knelt beside her with something new in his hands, a small chain. "Can I—please—can I just ask a question?" she pleaded.

"Yes."

"What was that? That you hit me with?"

"A rattan cane. And just so you know, I could have hit you with it a lot harder. That's not a threat. It's just the truth."

She swallowed. Tears threatened again. "Why...why are you doing this?"

He put one hand on her back, brushed across it soothingly. "Because I like to hurt you and make you do things. I really do, Kat. But do you know what?"

He leaned closer. Kat felt the brush of his dark hair against her cheek, the warmth of his forehead on her shoulder. "What?"

"I'll make it all worth it for you," he whispered. "I promise. Just bear with me. Okay?"

She shivered a little at the promise contained in his low, gruff voice. His hand slid from her back underneath to her breasts. He squeezed and caressed them, then pinched one of her nipples.

"This is going to hurt too. Brace yourself."

He reached under her with the chain. Just as it registered—that there were clamps on the chain, that they were going to be used on her nipples—pain blossomed where he touched her. The horrible clamp delivered hot hard pain that flared and settled into a dull ache. She hissed and tried to pull away from him but found herself arrested again by the inflexible web of rope.

"Please! Just give me a minute—"

He ignored her, moving to clamp the other nipple with the same horrible burst of pain. The chain hung down beneath her, cold and smooth against her knees.

"Please," she said again, but it wasn't a please begging him to remove them. It was a *please* of alarm, of confusion at the way she felt. She felt pain and terror and vulnerability and lust like a blanket over her. *I'll make it all worth it for you.* He put his hands on her back again, calming her. He ran fingertips down across her hot ass. *Please, please, please.*

He backed away, went to the desk, sat in the chair there. "Now, Kat, bring me the cranes."

She turned her head up to him. He was sitting, waiting. "But...how... I can't."

He looked at her a moment, then reached beside him to pick up the cane again. Kat's heart skipped. She lurched forward and picked up a blue one between her teeth, then shuffled forward making small sounds of panic. Her heart flipped over with relief as she heard the cane set down again. He reached for the paper figure and stroked her cheek as he took it. "Good girl. Bring them all."

It took awhile. She got better, over time, at moving and leaning. A few times she even managed to get two at once between her teeth. A couple times he chided her not to drool on them, an embarrassing reminder of just how turned-on she was. The way he sat and watched while she crawled around to do his bidding had her pussy aching.

She saw mostly cranes and floor, but every so often she raised her head to see his hairy calves, his knees with their sculpted muscle, his cock standing up hard and thick. In time she realized he was stringing each crane she brought on a length of fishing line. A bead at the end prevented them from falling off. She lost count of how many cranes she retrieved, but noticed him tie off one strand and lay it across the desk, beginning another. Her back and thighs began to ache near the end. He made soft sounds of encouragement as her energy started to flag. When she brought him the final crane, he took it and leaned to kiss the top of her head. She arched her neck to look up at him, then huddled on the floor at his feet, overcome.

His eyes, the way he'd looked at her. Pride and approval, affection and hot animal hunger. She laid her cheek against the carpet and wept.

The tears slaughtered him. She destroyed him.

She could have brought a knife and asked to kill him in that moment and he would have helped her plunge it into his chest.

He was out of the chair and draped over her back before he knew what he was doing. "Kat," he sighed against her ear. "Don't cry. You're such a good girl." She sobbed harder, great heaving sobs that pressed her back up against his stomach, the scratchy rope an irritant between them. *Release her, idiot.* He slid his hands beneath her, braced her, held her tight as he released the clamps. Her breath caught as the blood rushed back into her sensitive nipples. He went to work on the knots next, untying her with an alacrity that bore no resemblance to the slow, deliberate way he'd originally tied her. Her sobs weakened as he worked, diminished to intermittent sniffles. At last the rope loosened and slipped away. As soon as her ankles were free, she moved to get up.

"No." His voice sounded loud in the silent bedroom. His hands closed on her hips, held her still. "Don't move yet," he said more softly. "Give your body time to adjust slowly. And give me time to check you." She stayed still, shivering, not resisting him. He released her hips and reached for her hands, inspecting her wrists for cuts or chafing. He'd used soft rope but with beginners there was always a risk of damage. He was relieved to see only redness, no abrasions. He placed her hands on either side of her head and then moved down to her ankles. They were unblemished, no abrasions or cuts either. He circled them with thumb and finger, marveling at their shapeliness. Wondrous, compelling femininity.

"Okay," he said, reaching for her waist again. "Come here. Don't try to stand up yet." He pulled her into his lap and tucked her head under his chin. He held her—a huddled bundle—against his chest to warm her and felt the moisture still on her cheeks. "Okay, okay," he murmured against her hair. She moved one leg, pressed it against his throbbing erection. He was close to bursting for her. The bedside table was right there. He shifted to his knees, sitting back on his ankles. He reached over with one hand and got a condom from the drawer, still cradling her with the other hand. She was floppy, loose in his grasp, still in subspace. He ripped the condom wrapper open with his teeth and nudged her aside to roll it on. He positioned her slender body on the head of his cock.

He wanted to thrust deep, to yank her hips down onto him. He didn't. He eased into her, his hands all over her. Hips, breasts, back, stomach, every magical female plane. He took her face between his hands and thrust his tongue in her mouth, capturing her faint moan, a resonant secret. Her thighs tensed and she shuddered as he finally filled her completely. He tilted his hips, thrust upward so she took him to the very hilt. She twitched her hips and he groaned from the sensual tease, pulling her closer. Her arms reached for him, clasped around his neck as she plastered herself to his front. He began to fuck her. He wanted to possess her. He ran his hands up and down her back, pinching, scratching, massaging. Each small arch she made, each shivery undulation sent sparks of heat flashing to his pelvis. Soon he felt a feverish need for release.

"Oh," she sighed against his ear. "Ryan..."

With a growl he pitched forward and laid her on the floor before him. He splayed her legs wide and levered himself over her, pounding into her with his weight supported on his arms. Below him, she arched and met his thrusts with equal fervor, her arms thrown high over her head. She closed her eyes and he almost ordered her to open them, but then he felt her shudder and tense beneath him. He felt her walls grip him, contracting in rhythmic beats of ecstasy, an ecstasy reflected in her breathless pants. She did look up at him then. Her gaze dropped lower, to where he joined with her. The ache inside him broke wide and ambushed him. He climaxed with explosive force, emptying himself, jerking wildly in the harbor of her lovely, welcoming passage. He felt connected to her completely—mind, soul, nerves, organs, bodies. He fell over her, gasping.

"Holy fuck," he burst out against her shoulder. It was all he could think of to say.

He helped her up shortly afterward. They didn't speak right away, not about anything important. She tiptoed around as she prepared for bed. He haunted her space and she haunted his. They were both spooked.

"Should I... Do you want me to sleep here or in the other room?" she asked.

"Here. Naked. Just as you are."

She crawled under the covers and he slipped in beside her in the low light of the bedside lamp. She curled into a ball but he still pulled her against him. He held her so she couldn't scoot away. She stared off at something, her eyes distant and he watched her, wondering how she felt. She finally met his eyes. "It's so quiet here," she whispered. "I'll never be able to fall asleep."

He thought of her house, the crowded living areas, the room she shared with her nieces. He thought of his own quiet, sterile life.

"I'm so glad you're here, Kat," he said. *For a thousand reasons, I'm glad.* He turned off the lamp and held her close in the darkness. He thought he could hear her heart pounding away beside him. He heard her breath lengthen and grow even in sleep long before he so much as closed his eyes.

Chapter Eight

Kat was slogging her way through a horribly boring text on animal husbandry, trying to put thoughts of Ryan out of her mind. She had it bad for him. After two solid weeks of hedonistic pleasure, even translating passages about pigs fucking gave her a little thrill. She tried to focus, puzzling over a trick of phrasing. She hoped whatever Russian pig-farmers-in-training read this text appreciated her attention to small idiomatic detail.

She closed it right at five o'clock and headed home. His home. Her temporary home, where she felt more and more comfortable. He would be another hour at least, maybe later since it was Friday. She might do a half hour or so on his treadmill while she waited for him. Well, maybe twenty minutes. She'd get plenty more exercise later in bed.

He called when she was just finishing up to tell her he was bringing dinner home. He sounded pleased to hear she was exercising. He had an endearing preoccupation with her health, her eating and exercise habits. Well, it was kind of endearing but mostly exasperating. At first she'd pouted and resisted a healthier lifestyle. To her horror, his house was a no-junk-food zone. No chips, no cola, no candy, no coffee, not even any chocolate. Actually, he'd allowed her a little chocolate the week before when she was on her period. Otherwise, she'd told him bluntly, she would cut off his nuts while he was asleep. And she sneaked junk food at work for a while to get her fix, bought chips and candy out of the vending machine. He would never know, she thought.

But he knew. When he questioned her, she cracked and confessed. He spanked her, she cried, they fucked. Afterward he held her and caressed her, pouring warnings into her ear about the dangers of too much fat and high-fructose corn syrup. She heard nothing. She could only focus on his touch, his smell, the deep tone of his voice. Well, she heard something, she supposed, because his lectures were working. Just yesterday at lunch she found herself craving salad. Salad!

Last week, one day after work, she'd found herself snacking on *haricot verts* dipped in hummus. Hummus, for fuck's sake. And what the fuck was an *haricot vert* anyway? Some kind of rich doctor French green beans he'd turned her on to. She was always grabbing them out of his fridge.

There were other lessons, too, really intimate lessons about attention, pleasure and discipline. He touched her, grabbed her, stroked her and manipulated her. He tied her up regularly, practiced his "art" of shibari. She didn't totally get the art part or what he got out of it. She just knew it made her feel strange and nervous. She liked the fucking a lot more. She was even getting into stuff like going down on him. She was getting past her selfish impatience and starting to get into the ways she could make him react. He said anal was next. She was dubious but that never stopped him. If anything, it drove him on.

And he folded cranes every day. Sometimes just a few, sometimes a lot of them. Every time he did it she thought of that first night two weeks ago, when she'd crawled at his feet and fetched them one by one with her lips and teeth. He still strung them on lengths of fishing line, counting out groups of forty. He hung the completed strands in the corner, like a colorful waterfall. She didn't ask why. She knew why. He believed in wishes, fortune, fantasy. No wonder he got on so famously with her mother. They were two of a kind.

But not her, Kat thought as she ran on his treadmill. She didn't believe and she had no interest in learning how to fold them herself. But she still liked to look at them, the riotous colors, the way they moved and rustled slightly whenever the heater turned on. She was finding it easier to sleep in the silence. She was finding new, quieter noises to listen to just beneath the hum of her lust.

She was just getting out of the shower when he came to find her. She loved to see him after work, all doctor-y and businesslike. He would kiss her and she'd kiss him back and he'd begin the slow slide from brainy surgeon to horny lover. It always fascinated her. It melted her too.

While he changed out of his work clothes, she set out the food he'd brought, some Thai rolls and vegetable soup. She couldn't cook a lick, although she'd tried for him. He'd choked her meals down, then told her he didn't mind doing the cooking or bringing things home every once in a while. She loved him for that and she did what she could to contribute to mealtimes, which was set the table beforehand and clear it afterward so he had some time to relax.

Tonight after dinner Kat watched a little TV while he went over his medical notes and upcoming surgeries at his desk off the living room. When he finished he looked around at her. She was picking and fretting over a cut on her finger.

"What's wrong?"

"There was a paperclip incident at the office."

"Rusty paperclip?" His lips curved in a teasing grin. He was growing accustomed to her myriad mishaps and clumsiness. Weren't they together pretty much because she'd fallen down the stairs? He stretched out, his hands behind his head. "Don't mess around with it, doll. Let it heal."

She frowned. "I think I'm getting tetanus or something."

"I'm sure you are."

"I mean it. I had a headache earlier today and my jaw's been feeling a little achy. It could totally be lockjaw. What are the symptoms for tetanus?"

"I don't handle a lot of tetanus surgeries, to tell you the truth."

Fortune

Kat pursed her lips in annoyance. "Okay. Go ahead. Laugh all you want. If I get lockjaw where does that leave you? No more blowjobs."

He turned back to the computer and typed in some search terms with a sigh. "Hmm." He leaned his elbow on the desk, scanning the resulting pages. "Interesting."

"What? What are the symptoms?"

"Whining, frizzy hair and excessive paranoia."

"I hate you," she said. "You'll be so sorry after I'm gone."

"Come here." He turned to her, shaking with laughter. "Just come over here."

She went to stand in front of him. He gazed at her, his fingers reaching out to run over her fitted tee and up to her breasts. He cupped each one, then pinched her nipples though her shirt and sheer bra. She stood still the way he liked, not pulling away or flinching.

"Good girl," he said. "You know what I think? I think your aching jaw might be a symptom of something else." She smiled as his hands fell on her shoulders and he pushed her down with steady pressure. She knelt between his outstretched legs, unbuttoned and unzipped his jeans. He was already half-hard, his cock warm and heavy in her fingers.

"Jesus, Kat. Your hands are freezing. Just use your mouth."

She put her hands in her lap, scooted closer and took the head of his cock between her lips. She tasted the salty drop at the tip of it, gazing up at him. He sighed and leaned back, caressing her hair absently, his legs going slack on either side of her as she ran her tongue along his length. He was quickly filling her mouth, growing hard and rigid as she deep throated him. A great many of their lessons had focused on this and she was getting pretty good at it, if his moan was any indication.

"I'm sorry for your achy jaw, baby," he said. "But that feels like heaven. Don't stop."

She chuckled against his cock, teasing him with her tongue, pulling away to pay attention to the base of his shaft and his balls. She loved him this way. She loved that he was in her power for once. She loved the familiar taste and smell of his masculinity. It seemed an eternity ago she'd slept with men—a lot of men—and never once cared to kiss or touch their cocks. She couldn't get enough of Ryan's. In a couple weeks they could dispense with condoms altogether. They'd done screenings and she had already started the Pill. Some part of her understood what that signified, what it would mean even when the month was over. Monogamy. An end to her old whoring ways. So be it. He satisfied every need she had, so as long as he would keep seeing her, keep sleeping with her while she figured out her shit...

His fingers left her hair to rest on her temple. He stopped her with a soft sound and pulled out of her mouth. "Look at me." She raised her head to him, to his dark intense gaze. He traced his fingers down over her jaw to the sides of her neck. "I want to collar you."

She looked away, back at his cock. "What does that mean?"

"I want some kind of commitment. I want to collar you. I want you to be mine. Only mine."

She made an equivocal sound and put her mouth on his cock hoping to distract him, but he stopped her again. "Aren't you happy, Kat? Don't you like living here with me?"

She glanced up at him. Yes, she liked it, but she'd never intended for this to be permanent. She wasn't ready for this. "You said a month. That was the agreement."

"Agreements change. Life happens. Life is happening to us. My life is better with you and I know you like what we do together."

"Well, yeah. But it's been a couple of weeks. Yeah, okay. It's been fun."

His face twisted into a tight smile. "What an act. You kill me. Fine. Finish what you started, if that's all it is to you."

She looked back at his cock, her throat suddenly tight. Tears threatened and she didn't want them, not now.

"Go on," he said coldly. "Finish. Suck me."

She began to pull away. She'd barely moved an inch when his hand clamped on her shoulder. "Finish. Or I'll get the fucking whip."

She sat still, still as stone. She could safeword out of this moment. She knew she could even though she hadn't used a safeword yet. It felt like a safeword moment, but she didn't want to give him even that. She opened and took him in her mouth again, barely feeling it, just going through the motions. He was flagging, his hardness abating even as she threw herself into pleasuring him. Mindless technique. Tears rolled like liquid shame down her cheeks.

He made a sharp sound a moment later and pushed her back. He stood up and refastened himself, not looking at her. He went into his bedroom and slammed the door.

She, too, slammed the door on her way out.

* * * * *

Kat went home and pretended nothing had happened. Her mother and father played along and didn't ask any questions. She feigned exhaustion and went into her old room with her two nieces. She found it impossible to sleep with all the noise and lay awake long past midnight. Somehow she'd thought he would come for her. That he would ring the doorbell, come in, find a private place to apologize to her and ask her to come back.

But no. He didn't come. She barely slept at all, cycling in and out of short shallow dreams only to come awake with a start and look around for him. She wore her sister's clothes the next day because her clothes were at his place. She imagined at some point she'd have to slink back and get her things and deal with all that awkwardness.

She missed him.

The next evening her mother knocked on her bedroom door. "No, Mama," Kat said. "I don't want to talk."

"I do not care. We talk. You are sad for him, eh? What has happened? Why did he chase you away? Or...did you run from him?" she asked, astute as ever.

"He was too...he was too...he pushed for too much. Too much commitment. Plus he's just plain mean."

"Mean? What way is he mean? He hurt you? I kill him."

"No. Mama, you don't understand. Not mean like that. Just...annoying. Just forget it. It's not important now."

"Not important, eh?" Her mother scowled at her. "Then why you toss and turn? Why you skulk around with that sad face?"

"How do you know I toss and turn?"

"Mama knows everything. If you are sad without him, you must talk to him and explain how you feel."

"But I don't know how I feel. And I don't really want to talk to him."

"Hmph. Katyusha, you choose unhappiness."

"No. I choose freedom and common sense."

"Freedom to be alone and unhappy. Some common sense, this. *Ekh tyi*, always you have been this way. Do you know, I invite Dr. Ryan to dinner tonight."

"Mama!"

"He refused to come. He tell me, 'I would love to but...'" She looked at Kat in exasperation. "He says to me 'but,' 'but,' just as you do. 'But' this, 'but' that. This is too much 'buts.' Dr. Ryan, his 'but' is sad. I hear it in his voice."

"Mama, I love you but you're cuckoo."

"What is this, 'cuckoo'?"

"Crazy, weird. Lunatic. I don't want to see him, Mama. I don't care if his 'but' is sad. Just accept it. We don't work well together." The moment she said it, she knew it for a lie. She knew her mother knew too. Her mother could read anything on her face as if it were written there. Kat put her head in her hands. "I don't even know anymore, Mama. I don't know why I ran away. I don't know whose fault it was. I don't really care."

Her mama's fingers ran through her hair, rubbed her shoulders. "Why do you not tell him this? He probably feel the same way right now. Men. They do not know how to say what they feel sometimes. Do you think he is missing you, *zaika*?"

"No. Yes. I don't know."

She didn't know anything, only that a few moments later she said goodbye to her mama and papa and headed for the door.

* * * * *

Ryan drove home feeling as miserable as the cold, rainy weather. He worked late trying to forget her, to no avail. He wanted her to come back but he understood she might not. He hadn't folded a crane in two days.

He drove into his neighborhood and continued right through it, turned toward Brighton. He wasn't going to her house. He was just going to drive around looking at Christmas lights. The holidays were nearly here. His family and friends wanted to know his plans, wanted to invite him to parties and gatherings. For the first time in a long time he didn't want to go. He had imagined the holidays with her, imagined spending Christmas Eve introducing her to his parents, who would be home from Aruba. He had imagined the fun of spending Christmas Day in the hustle and bustle of Dmitri and Elena's home. Elena had called him this afternoon and invited him to dinner. He could have gone. Maybe he should have. He had a million questions to ask her, the seer, the fortune-teller. *Do we have a future? Is this worth fighting for?* He thought perhaps Elena could help him, but in the end he'd begged off with lame excuses and pretended he had a meeting he couldn't miss. Snow was starting to fall, tiny flurries that depressed him. He found himself idling in front of Kat's house.

The door swung open. The silhouette of a figure appeared there. He had a silly impulse to hide and an even sillier impulse to sit very still and not be noticed. It wasn't Kat anyway. It was her mother. She was beckoning him, barely cracking the door open in the cold. When Elena beckoned you obeyed. He turned off the car and walked up the sidewalk. She pulled him inside the door.

"Dr. Ryan."

"Mrs. Argounov, I know it's late—"

"Yes, you are too late. She is already going to your house."

"She is?"

"Yes, she is going back there now."

He turned immediately to go. Elena drew him back with a hand on his arm.

"Dr. Ryan, I tell you quickly. I have two answers for you." She looked into his eyes and spoke with a knowing intensity that shook him. "Yes. And yes."

* * * * *

When he walked in, he didn't see her. She wasn't in the living area and she wasn't in his room. He went to the other room, her room, and pushed the door open slowly. She was sitting on the bed fully dressed, her hands clasped in her lap. She looked over at him and it wasn't a happy or welcoming look. He thought, despite Elena's uncanny reassurances, that they didn't have a future after all, that she'd only come back to pack her things and leave him.

"Hello, Kat," he said softly.

"Hello."

He swallowed and cleared his throat. "How's your finger?"

She looked down, blinking rapidly. "I guess it wasn't tetanus after all."

"That's good to hear." He crossed to her, reached down for her finger and looked at the nonexistent injury. "In my professional opinion, this is going to heal up just fine."

She gazed up at him, the tiniest hint of a smile. "I'm glad to hear that."

"I'm glad you're here." He dropped her hand and ran his fingertip down the side of her cheek. "I'm sorry, Kat. I'm sorry I pushed you. It was wrong of me to try—to try to force you. I lost my temper, which is the worst thing a Dominant can do."

She looked down and away. "I... I'm sorry too." She stopped, wringing her hands together. "See, I..." She stopped again. Her face crumpled into unexpected tears. He knelt down and put his arms around her.

"Kat, don't cry. It's okay."

"No, I..." Her eyes met his then skittered away. "I just... You have to know... I don't know why I'm like this. I like you. I missed you. I really missed you. And..."

She drew in a shuddery breath. He rubbed her back and pulled her closer. "You don't have to explain. Don't feel you have to make excuses, because you don't. I'm your Dominant, yes, and you're my submissive, but you're still Kat. If you need time and space, I don't have any right to push you."

"But I— But I—" She took his hand, twisting it in her own. "I want you to push me. I need you to. Otherwise I'm too scared. I wanted— You know, the last two days, I wanted you to come drag me back."

He shook his head. "I won't keep chasing you. You can't keep running away. That's not how it's supposed to work."

She looked down again, wiped away the last of her tears. "I think I'm just too messed up for you."

"Yes. I've thought so all along," he teased gently. "But I can't stop hoping against hope that we can make this work somehow. I've been folding cranes, Kat. For a wish."

"For us?"

"Yes, for us."

She pursed her lips. "You know I don't believe that stuff."

"Yes, I know. Only one of us believes. But I still want you to stay. And I don't want us to limit things by arrangements and inflexible time frames. Let's just…live."

"Live?" She looked at him. "Does that involve…like…you know…"

"Lots of hot sex? Endless fucking? Tonight it will, anyway. Yes."

"Okay," she said with a tremulous smile. "Okay then. Let's live."

They started fucking right there in her bed, stopping midway to stumble into his room for a condom. Kat had never been fucked quite this way, simply fallen on and despoiled like a sacrifice. Instead of Ryan's staid walls, she thought there should be trees around them, wilderness and wildness. Fire and drumbeats. At least there was the multicolored mass of cranes in the corner, hanging down like leaves or vines.

"Can we fuck outside sometime?" she gasped in the middle of a particularly animalistic thrust.

"Yes!"

And they did fuck outside. He took her camping and they fucked huddled in a tent while snow fell over their heads. He took her to meet his parents—they were exactly as he described them to her—and they fucked. Well, upstairs. Later. In private. He gave her a collar for Christmas and they fucked. She never moved out and they never discussed the one-month agreement again.

Fortune

The first BDSM party came soon after the collar. It was a turning point for Kat, the point when she realized she felt more for Ryan than simple lust. The party took place at a dungeon downtown, a dark smoky space where everyone was half-naked—or totally naked—and no one seemed to have many inhibitions. It was a private party, invitation only, and it had a holiday theme. There was a kinky Santa giving spankings and lots of little elves running around wearing butt plugs and clamps.

Kat was nervous and overstimulated. She knew that Ryan knew all these people, but she knew no one at all. He held her hand tightly as he led her though the throngs. She had on the collar he'd given her, a simple black leather circle with a little lock on the back and an O-ring on the front. Normally it meant sex to her, Ryan's control and ownership of her. Now it felt more like protection. She knew Ryan's needs and wants and she trusted him. But there were a ton of other Doms around that she didn't know and didn't trust. Worse than that, there were a lot of subs and slaves she didn't like.

She didn't like them because of the way they looked at Ryan. They didn't just look at him. They talked to him, touched him and flirted with him. They all knew him. Most of them were a lot more scantily dressed than her. Ryan had approved of her little black dress and stockings but she felt childish next to the other women in their fetish wear. Maybe that had been his intention all along.

Aside from that, Kat got turned-on. When Ryan propelled her to the back of the space, to a bed with attachment points and vinyl sheets, she didn't resist.

He bent her over the footboard, which was obviously designed for fucking since it was at just the right height. He pulled up her dress to expose her naked pussy, her garter belt and black stockings. She could hear people coming over. She turned her head to see them staring at her bare, exposed girly bits. She almost lost her nerve then. Maybe he sensed it because he grabbed her collar and gave her a little shake. She buried her head in the vinyl sheets, hoping they were sanitized between uses. She tried to pull her legs together but he had an answer for that too. He took a spreader bar from the collection of toys mounted on the wall. It was her first time in a spreader bar. She nearly died.

The spreader bar took away the choice from her. The choice to resist, to close her legs and hide the shining wet secret there. She knew the slickness of her bare pussy would be obvious to anyone watching. And to Ryan. With all the spectators looking on, he cuffed her hands to the back of her neck using the ring on her collar. She was restricted and displayed. Helpless. She felt the familiar fall into subspace, not caring anymore who watched or what they thought.

Ryan slapped her ass with his hand a few times, warming it up. He left her, went to the wall to get an implement, returning with a broad black leather paddle. He put his hand on her collar again and leaned down close to her. "Are you ready?"

"Yes Sir." Her voice sounded dreamy and somehow resigned. A month ago she would have been agitated or whiny. She wouldn't even have been here. Now she arched back, wanting him, craving the pain.

"Owww!" She howled as the first stroke fell. She went up on her toes, trying to close her legs against the pain, but finding herself impaired by the spreader. Stinging heat bloomed across her ass cheeks. Another blow fell, and another. Her howls rose in hysterical volume. So much for subspace. He was hitting her too hard to find that escape. He put one hand on her back to quiet her, then spanked her again with the leather paddle. The broad surface impacted with a terrible sound and her ass flamed. Her hands clenched and unclenched behind her neck, twisting in her hair, but she found no solace. Another blow. *Owww...* She shook her head, wanting to cry, wanting to plead with him for mercy. Each blow was like fire, unbearable and awful. She let out a few small cries and gasps that made her feel a little better. Another blow, and another and then, finally, blessed numbness and resignation. She relaxed and let the pain overtake her, diffusing through her body like a slow running stream.

As soon as she relaxed he put the implement away, then stepped behind her and released his cock. She felt it spring free and fall against her heated skin. He didn't even take his pants all the way down. She felt the scratchy material of his dark jeans rubbing against her ass as he slid into her. Even with all the pain, she was amazingly wet. *Kat, you're an exhibitionist*, she thought. But no. It wasn't the fact that people were watching that turned her on. It was the fact that he was making her do this degenerate perverted scene. Because he wanted to. Because it pleased him. Or maybe to show off. She didn't care. Whatever it was, it was working for her.

Each time he entered her, stretching her walls and pulling her back by the hips, something animal inside her shivered. She moaned each time he filled her. She couldn't help it. In less than a minute she would lose control and have an orgasm. Her thighs began to ache from the strain of tensing and pulling against the inflexible spreader bar and her ass ached from the paddling. Her clit bumped against the footboard. She was going to come...she was going to...

He pulled her hair hard, a shock and a distraction. Her orgasm stuttered. His hand twisted harder, harder. She could feel only pain now, no pleasure. He pressed into her hard and bucked through his orgasm. She understood when he pulled out—understood with total clarity. *Not this time, doll.* She let out a broken sob of frustration. She didn't understand, but she was too overwrought to ask him why. She heard a few chuckles from the audience, a few catcalls.

"Yeah, make her wait for it."

"Good way to keep her worked-up."

Worked-up? She was beside herself. He undid her hands, undid the spreader bar and put everything away. He let her push down her dress. They didn't use condoms now, so she felt some warm liquid inching down the inside of her thigh as he drew her close and whispered in her ear.

"We're going to finish this at home, doll. We're going to finish it in your ass." Kat shivered, looking up into his dark eyes. She knew he'd wanted anal for some time now. It was a bit of a limit for her, not for any prudish reasons, but just because he was so damn large. "Trust me," he said.

"But..." she started.

"If you want to come you need to try it with me. I've decided the next time I let you come is while I'm in your ass."

The next time I let you come. So he would hold her orgasms ransom. Man, he was so good at this. He knew exactly how to manipulate her, because the way she felt right now, she was almost ready to beg him to pop her anal cherry right there on the icky vinyl bed. Instead she said, "Your cum is dripping out of me. I need to go clean up."

"No. I like the idea of it dripping out of you. My little cumslut. Let's go."

She rode home beside him, feeling too many feelings. She was frustrated but hot for him. She was nervous about trying anal sex. Worst of all, she was brooding about his kink history. Lord only knew how many submissives he'd been with before her. If the female attention he'd received at the dungeon was any indication, the number wasn't low.

"How many of those girls at the party have you slept with?" she asked, not quite able to sound casual.

"Jealous?"

"How many?"

"Quite a few. But it was just casual stuff, playing around."

"Hm." She crossed her arms over her chest, pressed her legs together more tightly.

"Good god. You really are jealous."

"Does that surprise you?"

"Actually, yes. Considering you've probably been with three times as many people."

"I have not been with three times as many people as you."

"I watched you leave with an awful lot of men from Masquerade."

"What do you mean, you watched me?"

"I watched you. I noticed you a long time before you noticed me. I watched you for a pretty long time, Ekaterina. You little slut."

Kat shook her head. "I noticed *you* a long time before you noticed *me*."

"No, I don't think so. Because I remember the first night you noticed me, despite your efforts to be slick."

"Yeah, you're so much slicker than me."

"In some ways," he smirked, pinching the top of her thigh. "Anyway, the point is, don't be a hypocrite. Yes, I've slept with other women. You've also slept with other men."

"But I don't see those other men anymore. Those women were all over you. And you seemed to enjoy it."

"So, so jealous." He glanced over at her as he turned the corner to their street. "Little Miss I'm-not-good-at-this, I-don't-want-a-relationship."

Kat fell silent. It was true. The "old" her hadn't felt these things. Jealousy. Possessiveness.

"Maybe your cranes are working," she joked, masking her unbalanced feelings in a teasing tone. "How many have you made so far?"

"Seven hundred and forty-five."

The number stunned her into silence. They were nearly home.

"Ready to get your ass fucked, Kat?"

She thought of him folding seven hundred and forty-five origami figures. "Um. Yeah. I guess I'll give it a try."

* * * * *

He got the rope first and tied her hands in a simple knot at the small of her back, running a line up to hook through her collar. Ryan thought as he worked that she was getting a lot better at tolerating the rigging. She was obviously still uncomfortable with it and still fought him a little, but not like she used to. At first, it was like roping a calf. Now it was more like gentling a filly. Sometimes she spooked but she was mostly okay.

When the knot was done and her hands were secure, he started with a plug. He bent her over the bed and held her down with one hand, slipping the slim toy inside her with the other hand, using plenty of lube. She whined and fidgeted as if he were torturing her. He had half a mind to get the next size up and see what she thought of that.

But no, he would go slow. He wanted her to like anal as much as he did, and a painful and frightening first experience wouldn't accomplish that. And of course he wasn't torturing her. She was just ultrasensitive and ultrahorny at the moment, which is what he'd intended when he didn't let her come at the club.

When the plug was firmly seated, he pressed the wide flange against her, pushing it deeper just to get a reaction. "How does that feel, naughty girl?"

"Naughty? I'm trying to be good. Why naughty?"

"Because I say so," he chuckled, slapping her ass. "And because you love what I'm doing to you right now."

She made some token sounds of disagreement, her hands pulling down on the rope that bound her, but he slipped a finger down to press against her sodden slit and her mutterings turned into a long sigh.

He chuckled again. She was such a hedonist when she got excited. He helped her up off the bed and made her stand straight and still before him, despite the sensation of the plug inside her narrow passage. "Okay, girl. This is how it goes. I'm going to lube up my cock really well and then I'm going to work it slowly into your ass, and then I'm going to fuck you. It will hurt like hell for the first few moments but just breathe through it, okay? As long as you relax, you'll survive."

"What if I don't survive?"

"I'll clean you up before I deliver your corpse to your parents."

Her outraged glare made him laugh out loud. "Look, you're going to fucking love this. Okay? So bend over the bed now and spread your legs."

She obeyed him, moving slowly. He noted the shiver and also the lust in her eyes. She bent over just as she'd been at the club but there was no spreader bar here. He stepped between her legs and acted as a spreader himself, pushing her feet even farther apart using his own. "Yes, just like that. Now stay."

She moaned softly as he removed the plug and tossed it on a towel on the floor for her to clean later. He generously lubed up his cock, then put another good-sized dab on her anus. He guided the head of his cock to her entrance with one hand, holding her waist with the other.

"Okay, this is the hard part. Just relax, even when you feel a little pain. It will get better."

He rocked against her, pressed in just a little, then out. The plug had stretched her a bit, but not much. She wiggled her hips and took a deep breath. With careful control, he pushed deeper, let his weight fall forward so just the head of his cock breached her. Her reaction was instant, a wail and a struggle. "No," he said sharply, putting both hands on her hips to hold her still. "Don't pull away. Relax. This is the worst of it."

"It hurts. You're hurting me."

"I know."

"You'll tear me!"

"No, I won't. Your body will adjust to it. Just..." He shifted in her ever so slightly, inching forward. "Just give it a minute." He rubbed her back, then leaned down to massage her shoulders. "You're my good girl," he whispered in her ear. "You're making me so happy. This feels so good, taking you in the ass. I've wanted this so badly." Again he inched forward with slow, deliberate care. "I love you like this, so horny and nasty. My nasty little sex toy. My little doll." He felt it, the instant she stopped fighting it and let her muscles relax. "Oh, yes...yes...you're so good." He slid deeper, grasping for control. She was so hot, so tight. The frantic, desperate noises she was making brought the animal inside him to life. He took her waist and slid in her to the hilt. She moaned as he drew out nearly all the way only to sink inside her again. Her hands struggled against the ropes and her hips twitched, fighting his control the only way she could. His feet kept hers spread. He leaned down, close against her, feeling her heat, her erotic electricity. He snaked a hand down her front and slid his fingers into her pussy, fingering her clit.

"What did I say earlier?" he asked hoarsely. "What did I say you could do with my cock in your ass?"

"Come! You said I could come."

She was arching her hips forward against his fingers, seeking the stimulation. Each jerk and arch launched an almost unbearable cascade of pleasure from his cock down into his balls and taint. "Yes...yes..." he said, thrusting deep, stroking her clit and then pinching it so she bucked even harder. "Come for me. Come with my cock in your ass."

She was nearly sobbing. He understood perfectly how she felt—his own arousal was reaching the breaking point. "Come, damn you. Come now. Come for me, you gorgeous little anal slut."

With a cry and gasp she let go, gave herself up to the carnal decadence, to the brute insistence of his possession. Her back arched. Her ass squeezed him and set off white-hot pulses of pleasure that exploded out of him and into her. He held her hands, pressing to her. Even bound, she managed to scratch the back of his palm in the throes of her uncontrolled ecstasy.

It was awhile before he untied her. For a long time he just lay over her back, nuzzling her neck and shoulders, whispering, "Good girl."

Chapter Nine
ಬ

It was an unseasonably warm day for early February. Still cold, but warm enough. Kat and Ryan were at her parents' home to celebrate her twin nephews' seventh birthday and the weather was so temperate they moved the party outside so the children could run around and play. Later they would need to leave to pick up Ryan's friends from the airport, a childhood pal and his wife with their young child. Kat was excited and a little nervous about meeting them since the guy, Dave, was Ryan's best friend. What if he didn't like her? And they were a Dom/sub couple too, Ryan told her. That freaked her out, but kind of fascinated her also. She wondered how other couples like them interacted on a day-to-day basis. So far, she'd just been stumbling along with Ryan's guidance. She had no idea if she was anything approaching a "good sub".

But for now they were awash in wrapping paper, punch and presents. The brothers-in-law milled around the barbecue, drinking beer and turning brats and kielbasa. They were speaking English for once in deference to Ryan. Kat watched, bemused, as her unflappable Dominant tried to blend in and act casual. Processed meats horrified him. She knew she'd have to listen to a diatribe about the evils of kielbasa all the way to Logan Airport.

While the men manned the grill, Elena circulated making sure everyone was having fun. Dmitri had long since retired with a headache. Children's parties were never his thing.

Kat sat on the other side of the patio with her sisters. They were like feudal festivals, these family gatherings, with the women and men separated. But it always happened because the men liked to talk men stuff and the women liked to gossip the way women did. Before, Kat used to drift somewhere in between, on the outskirts, feeling detached and unwelcome in either group. Not that anyone had actually excluded her... She just hadn't felt anything in common with them. Now her sisters huddled around her talking babies and husbands and work woes while Kat stared at Ryan and daydreamed about the night before.

He'd tied her up—again—the most intricate shibari yet. It had taken nearly an hour, not that she'd been keeping track. Watching his fingers, feeling the rope slide across her skin, waiting for his intent gaze to fall on her before it returned to the work at hand... All those sensory experiences had grown comfortable and familiar to her and were more than enough to keep her occupied and not bored.

He'd tied her on her back with her knees drawn up slightly, her wrists clasped to her front. He hadn't even bothered with the collar—she felt submissive and restricted enough by the confining design. He had used yards and yards of hemp rope drawn from his copious supply. By the time he was finished, every part of her was trussed into a neat, secure package. The front of her had been an intricate web of beautiful macrame, and the back an ingenious crisscrossing design. His fingers were so beautiful, so deft as he worked. She'd thought, at the end, that he was like some kind of spider spinning a web around her, ensnaring her.

She was truly caught.

One of her sisters, Irina, nudged her. "Katyusha, you're staring. I can't say I blame you," she added with a smirk. The other women emitted low teasing sounds of agreement.

Kat blushed and turned away, pretending innocence. "I'm just wondering when the kielbasa will be done."

Olga made a suggestive comment in Russian about hot sausage, which sent the entire group into gales of laughter. Ryan looked over at them and Kat waved back.

"He makes you happy," Zinaida said. It wasn't a question. Kat supposed it showed.

"Yes. He's a good man. He's very...focused. Patient. Kind." *Sexy. Funny. Trustworthy. Faithful. A genius.* When she enumerated all his qualities in her head she wondered why she couldn't let go of that last bit of self-preservation. Why she couldn't believe, even now, that everything would be okay. She still waited for disaster, still waited to lose interest. Still waited for heartbreak and devastation that never came.

He was folding paper now, using discarded gift-wrap to make origami animals for the children. They milled around him, asking for this animal or that, and each time he produced it precisely as asked, holding it out to the eager grasping hands with a flourish. The children laughed and always begged for another. He complied, manipulating the paper with the same agile fingers that had tied her into knots the night before. The children watched every movement, open-mouthed and astounded. Even this endeared him to her, this silly origami obsession. The production of cranes at home had waned somewhat, stalled in the eight hundreds. Perhaps he believed his wish had already come true. He smiled at the children, truly smiled as he interacted with them. Not the fake smile adults put on sometimes, but a true smile. The only smile she ever saw from him. He was so honest, so true.

And she was so fake.

Or maybe she wasn't. She didn't know anymore. She had pretended so long in her life that she still wasn't sure which of her feelings were fake and which were real.

"Auntie Katya," said one of the twins, running over. "Look what Dr. Ryan made me!"

"Hmm. Is that a flamingo or something?"

He laughed. "It's an elephant."

"Oh yes, I see it now." Kat gave the boy a hug and looked over at Ryan again. He was bouncing one of the toddlers on his knee now, trying to ignore the popping, fatty encased meats sizzling on the grill just across from him. She thought

Fortune

she might just die, her heart felt so much for him. She thought her chest might explode from what she felt inside.

* * * * *

"And that's why processed meat is so bad, Kat. I mean, no offense to your family, but I bet there are more toxins in one commercially produced serving of bratwurst than an entire course of childhood vaccines."

Kat put her hand over her mouth to stop herself from laughing, which would only rile him up more. She put on an air of innocent curiosity. "So, I mean... You know that for sure? What kind of toxins are you talking about?"

"Toxins like fat, chemical additives and preservatives—"

"Fat is a toxin?"

He gave a frustrated exhalation. "Well, yes, Kat. If you consider its adverse effect on health."

"Isn't fat on the food pyramid? So it can't really be a toxin. And all those fruits and vegetables you're always pushing on me, they're practically silly with toxic pesticides."

"No, they're not. Not the organic kind."

"The orgasmic kind?" She purposely misunderstood. "Like...cucumbers?"

"Kat—" He screwed up his face, trying not to laugh.

"Mmm...zucchini..." He was looking positively apoplectic. "So...what about stressing over what other people eat? Does that have any toxic effects on health?" She finally let out the giggles bubbling in her chest.

He shook his head at her. "You can laugh all you want, but I work with a lot of sick people. I take this stuff seriously."

"I know. I still like you though." She reached over and patted the hand that rested on his thigh as they cruised down I-90. He trapped it and squeezed her fingers against his palm.

"Don't you feel better now that you eat more healthy foods?" he asked.

"I do. But every once in a while, I just like to be…bad."

He finally smiled, relaxing. "I know that's the truth. Speaking of being bad, I expect you to behave yourself this weekend."

"Behave? Surely you jest." But her face clouded as she considered. "Do your friends… Do they follow a bunch of those… What are they? Protocols and stuff?"

"I'm not sure. I haven't seen them in a while, since last year. Dave's never been a real big protocol guy, but couples sometimes change over time. Look at how much more we do now than when we first started and it's only been a few months. If they do protocols we'll just deal with it."

"What about us?"

"What about us?"

"Do we just act…normal? I mean…"

"Do you want to do protocols, Kat?" he asked with a grin.

"No, I mean—"

"All this weekend, every time I cough that means you're to drop to your knees and take out my cock. Then when I blink four times, that means start sucking me."

Kat tsked.

"And of course," he added, "when I lay my finger alongside my nose, you know what that means."

"Um, you're going up the chimney?"

"No. Double penetration, silly."

Kat laughed but then sobered as his words sank in. Ryan cleared his throat, glancing over at her.

"I guess I should tell you that this is a couple I've played with. We all played together, just once, back before Dave and Sophie married. As it turned out, it was the weekend Hunter was conceived."

Kat raised her eyebrows. "Oh, really? Sure he's not yours?"

Fortune

Ryan laughed. "Pretty sure, since he's a mirror image of Dave and since it was Dave whose condom broke."

"What did you do?"

"Well, he actually forgot to tell her it happened, and then—"

"No, I mean... What did you do when all three of you played together? What kind of...activities?"

"We played some kinky games, had a lot of horny silliness."

"You double penetrated her? You and Dave?"

"Yes. But don't freak out, Kat. It was a fantasy of hers so we did it. I would never expect it of you."

She was silent, not sure whether she was scandalized, disgusted or horny as fuck about the idea of double penetration. "What...so what... What will you expect of me?"

He scratched his neck and thought a moment. "Nothing. I won't force you into anything. But have you ever been with more than one person at a time? Does it interest you at all?"

"Um... I don't... I mean...in what way?"

"In any way."

Kat thought about gangbangs, group sex, orgies. Then she imagined herself participating in something like that and her mind rebelled. "I don't know."

"Well, don't worry about it right now. If things happen, they happen. If they don't I won't be disappointed. I wasn't even going to bring it up."

"You were just going to spring it on me?"

"No. There are really no plans at all. Dave and I have never been planners. And like I said, I haven't seen them in a while. I don't know if he even still shares her. You're still pretty new to this so I'm not going to force anything on you that you don't want."

"But will you...if I don't... Will you still sleep with her? Without me?"

Kat's throat felt tight and her face felt hot as she asked it. *This is just more kinky weirdness,* she told herself. Like the spanking and the hardware and the shibari. Like the hummus and *haricots verts*, the twisted stuff she put up with in order to be with him.

He caught her hand again and brought it to his lips. "I won't sleep with her unless you're with me. No."

She let out her breath in relief, hoping he didn't hear it, hoping he didn't realize how jealous she felt and how much she really cared.

* * * * *

They had takeout pizza for dinner with their guests, a special treat. Kat liked the pizza she and Ryan made from scratch with whole-grain crust, organic sauce and low-fat cheese, but she'd forgotten how greasy and downright delicious real New York-style pizza was. They'd ordered it because the baby liked pizza. Little Hunter, who was not really a baby anymore but a headstrong toddler of one and a half. He chomped on his cheesy slice with his little toddler teeth and gums while Ryan, Kat, Dave and Sophie chatted and caught up. Conversation came easily. Before an hour passed, Kat's face ached from laughing at Dave and Ryan's interplay and their reminiscences about their boyhood craziness. Kat had been prepared not to like Dave, and especially Sophie, but she found them impossibly friendly. As a couple they were completely loved-up and connected, and they were wonderful, doting parents. When Sophie teased Ryan it just seemed fond, not flirty. When Dave talked to Kat she felt at ease.

She found herself, against all odds, thinking seriously about Ryan's suggestion that they might share a more decadent intimacy. There was no pressure and no expectation, just as he'd promised, but Kat found herself more and more attracted to Dave—and shockingly, Sophie too. Perhaps it was only because Dave was so much like Ryan. Not in appearance—Dave had longer hair and light hazel eyes that were nothing like Ryan's dark brown ones. No, it was Dave's secure, caring demeanor, his intelligence and humor that reminded her so much of Ryan. And Sophie was, really, so much like her. Quiet, dark-haired, with a tendency to introspection that Kat recognized in herself.

By the time Sophie left to settle the baby in his portable crib in the bonus room, Kat was nearly to the point of fearing something *wouldn't* happen. Ryan passed around beers, another rare treat for a special occasion, although he warned her with a wink that she would only get one. Kat barely drank it. She didn't care for beer. She just drank a few sips to take the edge off her nerves. Ryan and Dave seemed to be suffering from no such anxiety. They were working together to clear the living room, pushing the furniture to the walls and putting away the few breakable knickknacks. By the time Sophie came back down the men were sparring, facing each other across the cleared space with their legs braced apart. Both men balanced practically on their toes, light stalking menaces as they lunged for each other. They deflected blows so lightning-quick Kat didn't even notice them until one or the other had repelled it. Sophie returned to sit by Kat on the couch, leaning close to her with a chuckle.

"They're already at it, huh?"

"Do they do this often?"

"Every time," Sophie said. "They met in a karate class as kids. They've got some weird 'wax on, wax off' thing going on."

Kat erupted in laughter. Ryan looked over, momentarily distracted, and Dave capitalized by taking Ryan down to the floor in some kind of awkward grapple. The men struggled, hissing good-natured insults at each other. Kat had no idea who was winning, although Sophie whooped when the men flipped over in a convulsive explosion of movement. "Get him. Get him!"

"Why don't you come help me, O faithless one?" Dave gasped. "Instead of sitting there gabbing?"

Sophie laughed and crossed to the men and then Kat's mouth fell open as Sophie did a move with her leg that flipped Ryan over. He protested indignantly. "Double-teamed! No fair."

With a wicked grin, Dave rolled away and then Sophie—slight, submissive Sophie—actually put Ryan in a submission hold.

"Totally owned. Owned by my girl," Dave taunted. "Hell yeah!"

"Oh please," Ryan gasped, his face reddening from Sophie's chokehold. "I'm letting her win for a minute so her feelings don't get hurt."

"Lies—" Sophie yelled, just before Ryan broke her hold and flipped her over into an entirely different position of submission. Kat snorted, suppressing a laugh.

"Mercy," yelped Sophie. "Your elbow's on my hair."

"'Your elbow's on my hair,'" Ryan mimicked in a high-pitched voice, releasing her with pretended disgust. "Girls. Can't live with 'em, can't put 'em in an ultimate death hold."

"You can shove your ultimate death hold where the sun doesn't shine," said Sophie, stepping away and combing her straight black hair back to rights with her fingers, all feminine subby again. "We girls will watch from over here while you guys strangle each other, thank you very much."

The men went back to wrestling while Sophie picked up her beer again. Kat stared at her in awe. "Where did you learn to do that? That would sure come in handy around here sometimes."

Sophie smiled and shrugged. "Dave taught me. There was a guy... An ex-boyfriend he thought I might need some protection from. And he was right."

"Oh, I'm sorry."

"It all turned out fine in the end." The small shadow in her gaze brightened again. "It never hurts to know how to defend yourself and it's not hard to learn. I'm sure Ryan would teach you if you asked him."

"That might be fun."

"It's definitely fun. But yeah, to be honest, Ryan was just letting me beat him. I couldn't take him for real. He and Dave are pretty good at this stuff."

Kat looked down with a rueful smile. "Yeah. Ryan's so good at everything. Sometimes it makes me feel so…"

"Hopeless? Helpless? Pointless?"

"Yeah," said Kat in amazement. "Exactly."

"I used to feel the same way with Dave. It took me a long time to understand that he liked me just the way I was. Maybe it's a submissive thing, always wanting to be better for your Dominant. To live up to his expectations. When really, usually, their main desire is just for you to feel loved."

Sophie's words made so much sense and Kat was anxious to really talk to Sophie about these matters, about Dominance and submission and relationships while she had her ear. "How long did it take? I mean, for you to really feel at ease with each other? For everything to feel…sorted out?"

"Sorted out?" Sophie laughed lightly, a sweet musical sound. "You know, we still have to sort things out. Regularly. Having Hunter really threw a wrench in things. Not that we don't both love him to tears, but life has ups and downs. So do D/s relationships. What really matters is what's in here," she said, touching her chest.

Kat sighed. "My father says that exact same thing. But sometimes it seems so much more complicated."

"It is. It's definitely complicated. I guess all I'm saying is that as long as the love is there, and the will to be together, everything else works itself out."

Kat and Sophie noticed the quiet and stillness at the same time. They turned to find two pairs of eyes watching them — one dark, one light.

"Look," said Ryan. "A subby bonding moment."

"We're discussing what's more important," Sophie joked without missing a beat, "girth or length."

"Lucky for Kat, she has both," Ryan said, pulling Kat down to the floor.

Dave guffawed, moving up to sit beside Sophie. "I think we both know who has the King Dong here."

Sophie shook her head at Kat. "See? It always degenerates into this. Every time. They actually measured last time and they're nearly identical. Yes, they measured. Sad, I know."

Ryan laughed, rolling over so Kat was trapped under him. "She made us measure 'cause we wouldn't stop talking about it." Kat looked up into his dark, laughing eyes. It was so fun, so novel to see him like this—boyish, silly, at ease with his oldest friend. She tried to school her expression, tried to hide the jumble of her feelings, but as always he saw right through her. "Are you having fun, Kat?" he asked. She nodded and bit her lip. His thigh moved over hers to rest on her pelvis, pinning her to the floor. "Would you like to have more fun?"

She very much wanted to have more fun, but she couldn't quite bring herself to admit it out loud. She flicked a glance over at Sophie and Dave. They were watching from the sofa, their expressions equivocal and friendly. It was pretty clear to Kat that the decision was hers, that they were waiting for her to agree and say yes or demur and say no. She knew either way they would accept it. It was Kat who couldn't quite accept it yet.

"Answer me, Kat." Before her eyes, the boyfriend transformed, by degrees, into the Dominant. The face rearranged into more severe lines and the voice grew slightly deeper. "Would you like to have more fun? It's totally up to you."

She only paused a moment before she answered. "Yes, I would like to have more fun," she said quietly. "Yes Sir."

Chapter Ten

It was actually Sophie who undressed her when they went into the bedroom. Well, Sophie undressed first while Kat watched, too anxious to do anything but stand and shake. Then, looking at Sophie's pale, shapely body, her nervousness gave way to a sad curiosity. Sophie's body had scars. Lots of them. She remembered Sophie's words from before. *Dave taught me. There was a guy... An ex-boyfriend he thought I might need some protection from.*

"Dave didn't do this to me, Kat," Sophie said.

Kat shook her head, swallowing through the lump in her throat. "Of course not. No. I'm... I'm sorry to stare. I'm just...sorry." Kat thought about her own "problems", her self-absorption and petty ennui. She thought with shame that her problems were nothing beside the pain etched in Sophie's skin.

Sophie smiled and shrugged. "I'm over it. Ancient history. I'm okay now."

While the girls talked quietly, Ryan and Dave pulled the comforter off the bed and then went through Ryan's drawers sorting through various implements and toys. Paddles, whips, nipple clamps, cuffs and dildos were tossed onto the bed. Sophie took off Kat's shirt and bra and then helped her shimmy out of her jeans.

"It will be so amazingly fun. You'll see," she reassured Kat with a sparkle in her eyes. "It's almost too fun when the two of them get going."

"I bet." Kat's voice sounded tight even though she wanted to sound casual, to take it all in stride as easily as Sophie. Group sex wouldn't be easy for her but she still wanted it. She was scared but she was hot. She looked at Sophie apologetically.

"If they want us to do stuff together... I'm not a lesbian. Or even bi really. Nothing personal."

Sophie laughed her light tinkly laugh. "I'm not either. It won't matter. I'm sure they'll be mostly interested in burying their cocks in us. And if they ask us to do things together, we'll just do it. You know. 'Yes Sir' and all that stuff."

Kat laughed. "Okay."

"Did I hear a 'Yes Sir' over there?" asked Ryan. "All right, girls. The men could use some fluffing."

In Kat's opinion, neither man appeared to need fluffing, but she moved anyway to kneel at Ryan's feet.

"No, we'd like some girl-on-girl fluffing," Ryan clarified with a grin.

"Damn right," Dave agreed. "Girls fondling each other. Turning each other on."

Kat and Sophie traded exasperated looks. "So much for my theory," Sophie said out of the side of her mouth. Kat let out a wild giggle before she could stop herself.

"Silence, wenches," said Dave. "At least kiss or something."

Sophie reached out to Kat first with an encouraging smile. Kat had never kissed a girl, never wanted to. When Sophie's hand came to rest on her waist, the light, soft touch startled her. It was so unlike Ryan's usual urgent grip. Kat moved closer, slid her own arm around Sophie's waist, their hips brushing together. Sophie's skin was so smooth and she felt so delicate. With a kind of fascination, Kat inched forward and touched her lips to Sophie's. They kissed, just a peck at first, then a more tentative exploration. They were both so nervous that their teeth knocked together with a dull sound. Kat snorted and Sophie erupted into hysterical laughter. Dave and Ryan exchanged feigned looks of derision.

"So sad," Dave said.

Fortune

"Poor excuse for hot, sexy lesbians," Ryan agreed.

Kat and Sophie tried to stifle their laughter, stepping apart as the men turned to the arsenal on the bed. Dave and Ryan consulted behind their hands, disagreeing, then nodding, everything in secretive whispers. Ryan stood and rooted through another drawer for a different pair of nipple clamps, clover clamps with a longer chain. He showed it to Dave with a smile, then approached the girls. "One end of this on each girl. Put the clamps on each other," he said. "Sophie first."

He handed Sophie one of the clamps. She glanced up at Kat from under her lashes. Kat hated the clovers. They hurt more than the usual clamps and she knew from experience that they tightened even more when yanked upon. She closed her eyes and braced. Sophie played with her nipple a little and then attached the biting clip. Kat moaned and shifted from foot-to-foot, trying to work though the pain that assailed her. When she'd caught her breath and collected herself again, Sophie handed her the other clip. Since Sophie had clamped her left breast, Kat knew to clamp Sophie's right. She pinched her pink nipple until it stood out taut and crinkled and then, with a feeling of dread and excitement, closed the clamp on the other woman's tender flesh. Sophie reacted similarly, a gasp of pain and then a slow relaxation. She took Kat's hand and squeezed it with a smile.

Ryan and Dave stared and Kat stared back, feeling a strange kind of feminine power. Her nipple ached and Kat realized the perverse dilemma the girls shared. Any movement to pull away from Sophie would tighten the tether between them and torture both girls even worse. So they stood together, submissive sisters. Dave and Ryan began to plot again.

"Ass plugs, I think," said Ryan.

Dave nodded. "Absolutely. Right now."

The men stood and collected butt plugs and lubricant. Kat whined softly as Ryan worked the plug he'd chosen into her ass. It wasn't the slim one, but one of a slightly larger size.

Since she was standing, the insertion was more difficult and vastly more uncomfortable. She took deep breaths and willed herself to accept the invasion. Beside her, she could feel Sophie fidgeting and tensing too. By the time the toy was fully seated inside her, her whole body was settling into a thrum of arousal. Her ass clenched around the blunt object and her nipple ached from the clover clamp. The men sat side by side on the bed then. Dave reached for the chain between the girls and pulled.

With a squeak, Kat fell to her knees in front of her lover and Sophie sank down beside her. Sophie was already caressing and kissing Dave's cock. Kat looked up at Ryan and he smiled at her, that sexy grin that told her he was having fun. He pulled her head down and she began to fellate him, lust and excitement mounting in her. His soft groans and whispers egged her on. Beside her, she felt Dave's knees against her shoulder, bumping her now and again, and Sophie's body right next to her. When either girl moved too far to one side, the chain between them grew taut and the resulting pain made Kat even hornier and more eager to please. After what might have been an hour or maybe only five minutes, the men stopped the girls. Kat watched, breathless, as they produced flavored condoms, casually rolling them on. The import of a condom for oral didn't occur to Kat at first, not until the men switched sides.

Kat tried not to freak out and freeze up. Ryan chucked her under the chin and smiled over at her. "Just like me, doll. Only just a little smaller. And cherry-flavored."

Sophie giggled and then Kat giggled too. Dave rubbed Kat's shoulder and said, "He's a liar. I'm bigger." Sophie sniffed Ryan's cock and said, "Smells like banana." And then everything seemed okay. Kat gave herself up to the fun naughtiness of what they were doing. She and Sophie set to work pleasuring each other's mates. Kat was surprised at how different it was to suck off Dave. For men so much the same everything was different—scent, reactions, exhalations, the feel of his fingers in her hair. It excited her that she was able to pleasure him so easily. When he came with a growl, clutching her curls, she felt a true sense of pride. She heard Ryan gasp, "Kat wins."

"This time," Dave said, stroking Kat's cheek. Kat looked over at Sophie, watched her bring Ryan to climax just a minute or so later. She felt no jealousy, only a crippling horniness. The nipple clamp still pulled at her sore nipple, her ass still throbbed from the plug lodged there and her clit ached for satisfaction.

"What should we do with them now?" asked Dave when he caught his breath. "They still look pretty worked-up."

"Maybe we should fuck them senseless."

"I'm totally on board with that plan. However," Dave added, "it's going to be a few moments before King Dong is ready to go again."

"Yes. It's too bad for them. They look pretty hornified."

Kat looked up at Ryan, embarrassed and yes, dying to come, to get fucked, to get edged...anything.

"Let's paddle them for a while. And crop them too," Ryan suggested brightly. *Damn. Anything but that.*

But Dave agreed that paddling and cropping them would be a great idea. He also suggested that they shouldn't leave the clover clamps on too long since they were pretty powerful. Kat was greatly relieved to hear that until he went on to suggest they simply move them to the other breasts. Again, the girls were made to stand and clamp each other. This time was even worse because Kat's other nipple was still singing with the agony of release when Sophie clamped the torturous device to the second nipple. Kat began to think that Ryan and Dave together might possibly be overkill as she clamped poor Sophie. Once they were tethered again, they were made to lie together side by side on the bed, flat on their stomachs with their arms over their heads.

Immediately Kat realized that even a slight shift would pull the chain between their nipples and result in some serious discomfort. Sophie realized it too and looked over at Kat with wide eyes. For now, it was fine, but when they were paddled...

"It's called predicament bondage," said Ryan, giving Kat a quick crack on the ass with the crop. Her unconscious jerk resulted in a plaintive "ouch" from her fellow sub and a sharp pain in her own nipple. "Ryan! Sir...please."

"I suppose this would be as good a time as ever to start working on self-control and not trying to evade me. Don't you think?"

"Yes Sir," said Kat. Dave brought the paddle down on Sophie's ass with a whack. It was so close to Kat that she flinched and then she felt the tug as Sophie lurched in agony. "Sorry," Sophie whispered after the fact.

"It's okay. Ow!"

The two men commenced to belabor their subs' bottoms. Kat fisted her hands above her head as she tried not to reach behind her to deflect the blows. Ryan cropped her first while Dave paddled Sophie. Each time she twisted her hips to the side, she heard Sophie's gasp and felt guilty about it because Sophie didn't tug her breast nearly as much. After a few minutes, the men took a break, exchanging implements. Kat lay still, staring over at Sophie. Sophie smiled at her faintly but they didn't talk. Kat was half in and half out of subspace. The throb in her ass wasn't too unpleasant when fresh blows weren't landing. There was just an overall warm tingling adding to the heat already overflowing between her legs. The plug still felt as if it was stretching her. Being plugged was usually a sign that Ryan intended to use her ass. Or perhaps...perhaps both of them would have a turn. The idea made her shudder with a kind of delicious fear. By the time the men recommenced, Kat was struggling not to grind her hips against the bed because she knew Ryan would hit her harder if she did.

Fortune

Above their heads, Sophie reached for Kat's hand and grasped it. Kat steeled herself under the punishing paddle strokes and disciplined herself to stillness. She tensed her muscles, trying hard to breathe through the stinging slaps rather than attempt to evade them or pull away in pain. The men talked back and forth to each other but their words barely registered. If they spoke to her she didn't know it. All her energy was going into being still in the haze of her erotic torture. At some point she began to cry, whether from stress, horniness or basic overstimulation, she didn't know. She wiped her tears against the sheets, not wanting to move her arms and get in trouble. Beside her, Sophie was more stoic, her face screwed into a mask of resignation. Maybe someday, thought Kat, she could handle pain that way.

At last the men stopped, inspecting the girls' bottoms. Kat felt her ass cheeks squeezed, fondled, parted—by whom, she didn't know. It felt as if both men were touching her. She still didn't move, didn't dare pull away in her predicament. In short order, the clamps were finally removed and for that, at least, Kat breathed a sigh of relief. But the plugs stayed in and the girls were made to stand. Then, to her surprise, the men decided to part ways and fuck in separate rooms. The surprising thing was, she was sent away with Dave.

She followed him down the hall, wet and horny enough to concede to anything. If it had to be Dave to make her come, she'd take Dave in a heartbeat and happily give Sophie to Ryan. Anything, anything to assuage the maddening ache. Dave led her into the other bedroom, leaving the door open. He flicked all the lights on.

"I'm a photographer," he said with a lopsided smile. "Lights are my thing. Come here, Kat."

Kat went to him, trying not to let her apprehension show. He tilted her face up to his in the light. "You're okay with this?"

His cock was poking against her front. He had a condom in his hand so she knew he would use one. She nodded. "Yeah, I'm just a little..."

"Scared?"

"No..."

"Horny?"

"Yes."

"I'd be happy to help you with that." He ran his knuckles down one side of her jaw, scrutinizing her. Checking for true consent?

"I...you... I'm happy to serve you, Sir," she stammered. She thought it was a good enough speech and he smiled at her indulgently.

"I bet you're happy to. I was actually just thinking about how lovely and pure your face is. Perhaps Ryan will let me photograph you sometime. I hope so."

Lovely? Pure? All Kat could think of was sinking down to the floor and begging for sex. As if he could read her mind, he yanked her down with rough, abrupt insistence. He parted her legs and cupped her pussy. She burned with sudden humiliation as his fingers grazed the edge of the buttplug. He noticed her embarrassment—how could he not notice everything in this light? "It doesn't come out right now," he assured her. "Later Ryan wants your ass. But for now, I'm going to take your pussy."

I'm going to take your pussy. She gazed up at him in curiosity. He was so different from Ryan. Had she ever imagined they were alike? But it was exciting being with this near-stranger because she trusted him implicitly. She knew Ryan would never have sent her away with someone he didn't trust. Ryan had told her he wouldn't sleep with Sophie unless she was with him. And truly, she was with him. They were in this together, even if he was a room away with a different girl. She looked up at his friend, not trying to hide all the lust and horniness she felt.

"What do you want, Kat?"

"I want you to fuck me. Please, Sir."

He spread her legs wider, rubbed her clit, then rolled a condom onto his rigid cock, positioning himself at her entrance. He pressed in slowly and Kat quailed from the intense feeling of fullness. The plug shifted in her ass as Dave's cock parted and filled her pussy. He groaned, arching over her braced on his arms. "You're so hot, Kat. You feel so fucking awesome..." Kat couldn't reply, couldn't speak. Dave moved in her with long steady strokes that resonated deep inside. She felt somehow ashamed, unfaithful, because she was already close to coming. The novelty of a new lover, the buildup of the last hour, the teasing, the predicament bondage with the nipple clamps, the plug in her ass making her feel reckless and naughty — and now this. The hard cock invading her, subduing her. Dave's balls smacked against her slit and her sore ass slid across the scratchy carpet each time he moved into her again.

"Oh...oh god," she moaned helplessly.

"Mmmm..." hummed Dave in agreement. "Come on, Kat. Come for me. Come hard. Let it all go. I want to see what you look like when Ryan makes you come. He makes you come, doesn't he?"

"Yes! Oh yes, yes!"

"Now I'm making you come too. Come, and I'll tell him what a good girl you are, what a sweet slutty girl..."

His words gathered in her ears, slipped down over her body and made her entire pelvis throb. She pulled her legs up, arched her back beneath him.

"Yeah," he whispered, urging her on. "Come for me, I want to see it."

Her desire reached a fever pitch and she gasped in desperation. "Oh god, yes, yes, yes..." The last *yes* broke and faded as her orgasm overtook her. Her entire middle seemed to contract on the hard intrusions inside it. Dave pounded into her, gasping, his own yeses spilling forth as he buried his head against her hair. He slowed finally and gave a little shudder inside her. Carefully he pulled out, discarded the condom, then returned to where she lay completely insensible on the floor. He propped himself up on one arm next to her, smiling down at her.

She gazed back at him, feeling shy suddenly. How ridiculous to feel shy and coy at this point, but she did. "Do we go back now?" she asked.

"Not just yet. Haven't you ever heard of aftercare? Does that bastard Ryan fall asleep thirty seconds after you're done?"

Kat giggled. "Most of the time it's me falling asleep in thirty seconds."

"You remind me a lot of my Sophie. She really likes you. I can tell. It's good for her, being around someone else who understands the lifestyle, who lives the same kind of dynamic she does."

Kat nodded. "It's good for me too. I'm actually pretty new at this."

"Yes, Ryan told me he'd corrupted a vanilla. It doesn't always work. It's nice that you took to it."

"Was Sophie vanilla when you first met her?"

"Oh, no. Sophie was a longtime player, just like me. But she'd gotten into a kind of...situation."

"I gathered that," said Kat. "Terrible. Did the guy who did it...did he..."

"He's rotting in jail now. Hopefully for a good long time." A pall fell across Dave's face. "He tried to kill her. You have to... In this lifestyle, Kat...you have to be careful. You have to only play with people you trust. I really hope things work out long-term for you and Ryan, but if they don't—if you move on to another person—just take care."

"I will. Definitely. Not that—"

Dave laughed. "Yeah. Don't tell Ryan I'm giving you advice on what to do after you leave him. He's pretty hooked on you."

Kat blushed. "I... I really like him too."

"Do you? He's a great friend of mine. He's solid." He looked down at her very thoughtfully. "I shouldn't pry. I don't mean to. But I mean, things are pretty good with you guys?"

"Well, sure. I mean...it's still early. We just met a few months ago."

"He told me about your fall down the stairs."

Kat rolled her eyes. "Does he tell that to everyone? 'Here's my new girlfriend, Kat. I met her when she fell down the stairs.' Anyway, we met before that." She laughed softly. "And I was so sure he was totally full of shit."

"Sometimes he can give that impression."

They both fell silent. It didn't escape Kat's notice that all she and Dave had really talked about were each other's partners.

"Well, I guess we should get back," Dave said. "See if Ryan's done rogering Sophie yet."

"Rogering?" Kat laughed as Dave helped her up with an outstretched hand. When they got back to Ryan's bedroom, he and Sophie, too, were chatting on the floor. Ryan looked up as they entered.

"Hey Dave, Sophie says she thinks my cock is just a little bigger than yours. Didn't you say that, Soph?"

"Ryan!" Sophie scolded. She turned to Dave. "I did not say that, honey."

"Whatever," said Dave. "Either way my cock's going in your ass, woman."

The girls were sent into the bathroom to take out their plugs and lube their assholes. Kat was pretty sure this was the weirdest thing two girls had ever done while going to the bathroom in pairs. Kat blushed the entire time she took care of business, but Sophie just looked over at her and said, "Anal rocks!"

Back out in the bedroom, Ryan and Dave were chatting while they waited. They looked up as the girls entered. "C'mere, Kat. Get me hard. You have one more hole to fuck," said Ryan.

"Well, I mean, you don't have to fuck it if you're too tired," Kat said.

Sophie and Dave snickered as Ryan pulled Kat over his lap and started whacking her bottom. "Ouch," she howled, kicking her legs. "Okay, okay. We can fuck then."

"Beg me," Ryan teased, pausing with his hand over her ass. "Really nice. 'Please, Sir, fuck my ass.'"

"Please, Sir, fuck my ass."

Sophie chuckled as Dave bent her over the bed. She called over to Ryan, "Please, Sir, fuck her ass."

Kat pretended outrage. "Whose side are you on?"

"Good girl," Ryan nodded at Sophie, just as Sophie moaned from Dave driving into her from behind.

Ryan slapped Kat's ass one last time, then pushed her down on the floor on all fours, knelt behind her and gripped her hips in two strong hands. "I hope you lubed yourself up good, little girl."

"Yes Sir," Kat replied. The growly, stern tone in his voice made her feel very submissive—as did the feel of him pressing the head of his cock against her ass. His hands roved down her back, kneading and scratching her. Sophie's soft moans and Dave's grunts faded into the background as Ryan worked the head of his cock past Kat's clenching sphincter. Her whine rose to a cry as he drove forward. He stilled inside her, rocking back and forth slowly. Kat was up on her knees, ass in the air. If Ryan hadn't been holding her, she would have collapsed from the sensation of his cock filling her ass. It felt like pure debauchery and she loved it. Sophie's groans and cries in the background only fueled Kat's lust. Ryan, too, seemed caught

Fortune

up in the moment, fucking Kat hard, then soft, then so deep she moaned and jerked away from him.

He fucked her for a long time, asserting his dominance, subjecting her body to his will. Dave and Sophie finished first with noisy climactic groans. But Kat's orgasm arrived on a slow-simmering arc that seemed to engulf her rather than consume her. Ryan leaned over her, driving into her firmly and deeply, with slow exhalations against her ear. Her knees slipped and spread wider on the carpet. He followed her down, still holding her hips. She arched, she grasped, she abased herself for him and like rolling, unexpected thunder from a distance, her climax came. She gave a long, drawn-out groan as it shook her. She felt her body turned inside out, given completely over to his intimate possession. Soon after, he collapsed over her, his rough, hairy chest against her back. They spooned together for a while, Kat counting her heartbeats above his quiet gasps. Her mind drifted. She did not attempt to make sense of the evening's activities, only reflected that they were now definitely over. She felt completely fucked out. She couldn't have moved if she had to. She didn't move for fifteen minutes or so, until Ryan suggested a shower and the girls gratefully agreed.

All four of them climbed into Ryan's oversize shower, a laughing, exhausted tangle of slick bodies jockeying for position under the warm, soothing stream. Kat thought then that what they'd done wasn't perverse or wrong at all—it was just fun. Some couples got together and played Bunco, while other couples got together and fucked. Kat thought Bunco was lame anyway.

After they got out of the shower, after Sophie checked on baby Hunter, they all tumbled into bed together naked, the girls snuggled together between the guys. Sophie and Dave fell right to sleep but Kat was restless. Finally Ryan leaned down to whisper in her ear.

"Baby, everything's okay. You're mine, always. Even when I share you."

"I know." Kat shifted closer to him, snuggled against his broad chest. "It's just…"

"Just what, baby?"

"When I was in the other room with Dave…"

"What?" Ryan shifted to look down at her with concern in the darkness. "Did something happen?"

"No, I just… I really…enjoyed it. I mean, I came pretty hard with him."

Ryan chuckled softly. "I came with Sophie too. It's okay. That's how it happens when you swap. I'm glad you had fun. You did have fun, didn't you?"

"Yes. I just feel a little weird though. A little dirty."

His hand grazed her nipple and then moved lower. "That's because you are a little dirty. A *lot* dirty. Now get some sleep. And try to dream about me, not Dave and the epic orgasm he gave you."

Kat giggled. "What if I dream about Sophie?"

"Ahh…" whispered Ryan. "If you dream about Sophie, I want to hear all about it in the morning."

"Yes Sir," Kat whispered back with a smile.

Chapter Eleven

The next day the baby was up early. Dave was up early too, off to his photography convention. Kat lay in bed, every muscle aching, before Ryan finally rousted her to have breakfast. He made a big fuss about rehydrating her, teasing her about all the "moisture" she'd lost the night before. Sophie and Kat chatted and took Hunter for a walk while Ryan puttered around the house relaxing.

Hunter was endlessly fascinating to Kat. It wasn't that she didn't already have a zillion little cousins just like him. It was that the little boy was Dave and Sophie's child, and Dave and Sophie were just like them. Kat let herself imagine for the first time that she and Ryan might someday make a baby. The idea terrified her, but at the same time she caught herself wondering what it would be like. Ryan would be a spectacular father. Kat as a mother... Well...she just didn't know.

That night Ryan got called into the hospital for an emergency surgery. Without him there was no talk of playing again. After Hunter went to sleep, they played cards and Kat discovered that Sophie was quite the poker shark. It felt okay not to do another scene. After all, they'd played so hard the night before that another encounter so soon might have been a letdown. Kat let herself just enjoy Dave and Sophie's company. She hadn't had a really good, close friend in so long and had certainly never enjoyed the novelty of having "couple friends". When they put the cards away, Sophie and Kat sat together on the couch just talking. Sophie asked all the tough questions. It wasn't Dave who would size up her suitability for Ryan, as it turned out. It was Sophie.

"You know," Sophie said. "I have to tell you. I've never seen Ryan this way."

"What way?"

Sophie paused, considering. "In love."

Kat made a soft sound, maybe a laugh, although she felt alarmed. "I don't know, Sophie. We've mainly been doing this D/s stuff. I'm not even very good at it yet. Maybe...as time goes on..."

"He's in love with you. Hard in love. Kat, I know Ryan. I know he's all about self-control and lectures and drinking soy milk and all that crap. He can be...hmmm... What's a nice way to say this? Uptight. But I've never seen him like this. So possessive and crazy for a girl. So...monogamous." Sophie grinned. "He used to be all about 'love 'em and leave 'em'. I'm not kidding. He was a real manwhore, just into playing with the Barbie sluts. But he's different now. So different. The way he is with you...the way he looks at you..."

Kat blushed, glancing up at Sophie. "He's folded over eight hundred cranes for us. Something about good fortune. I can't imagine why."

"Can't you?" Sophie shook her head with a rueful smile. "I guess I felt the same way with Dave. 'Why me? What did I do to deserve this? He can't really like me.' All those questions screwed-up girls like us ask."

Kat laughed. "I know. It's terrible. It's not that I question what he wants. I just wish I knew..."

"Knew what? How everything would turn out? I don't know that anyone really knows that. Unless you're a fortune-teller or something," Sophie snorted.

Kat bit back a smile. "Yeah. Everyone knows that's a load of bull."

"Exactly. You just have to be brave. And you have to trust your Dominant. Ryan is trustworthy, Kat, believe me."

I know he's trustworthy, she wanted to say. *I just don't know if I am.* But she held her tongue and sat still, wishing she was Sophie, settled and secure instead of scared and conflicted.

Fortune

When they all said their goodbyes at the airport the next morning, Sophie hugged her and whispered in her ear, "You make your own fortune, Kat. Don't let him get away."

* * * * *

Kat was quiet all the way home from the airport. Ryan wondered if it was tired-quietness or problem-quietness. "Okay, doll?" he asked, trying to sound casual.

"I'm fine," she said, turning away from him a little.

Problem-quietness. Yep. "So what did you think of the weekend? Of Dave and Sophie?" he asked lightly.

"They were really nice. Fun. Their baby was adorable."

He couldn't draw much more out of her. Back at home, he stripped her in the bedroom and got out rope. She wasn't really in the mood. He wasn't sure he was either. Last night's emergency surgery hadn't been a success, and the weekend as a whole had brought up feelings for him that he wasn't quite prepared for. It was somewhat difficult seeing Sophie and Dave so peaceful and content with their little child and successful marriage. He wondered if he would ever find the same with Kat and then he felt guilty for having those disloyal feelings at all. He thought perhaps he should start folding cranes again, although he knew, realistically, that folded paper wouldn't save them if they weren't meant to be.

But he kept all these feelings to himself as he tied her. She already doubted enough. If he voiced his own doubts on top of hers he knew she would bolt. He handled her gently as he decorated her body with the rope. He looped it around her nipples, just enough pressure to tease her. He placed a knot on her clit. She watched him with a purposely secretive gaze. Whatever thoughts and issues she was struggling with remained, as usual, unvoiced and hidden. He pulled the rope more tightly between her crotch in a fit of pique.

"What is it, Kat? Talk to me."

"What?" She sounded defensive.

"What are you upset about? You didn't like playing with Dave and Sophie?"

She shrugged. "I liked that part." He met her eyes.

"Then what?"

She swallowed, bit her lip. He thought he saw her throat work a little. Was she going to cry? His hands stilled on the rope.

"Please talk to me," he said. "For once, just say what's on your mind."

"I was just talking to Sophie...yesterday..." Again her lips trembled.

"About what?"

"She said you loved me. She said she knew it."

He smiled softly. Any other girl would have been gooey over it. Kat looked about ready to spit. "Of course I love you," he said. "Surely you knew that. I've never said it because...because of how you are. Because I knew it would upset you. But you had to know."

"I don't know what I know."

He touched her cheek softly and her eyes closed. "You always say that. But I think you do know."

She started to struggle then. Her hips twisted and her arms pulled in their weblike rope bonds. "Please untie me."

"No."

"If we were like them, with a baby, all married and stuff," she said angrily, "then you couldn't do this anymore. This stuff you love so much. You couldn't get naked and tie me in knots—"

"It wouldn't matter."

"And fuck me whenever you want and...and have your friends come over and—"

"Kat. It wouldn't matter. I would be happy just to be with you, just to love you. I love you." He leaned over her where she twisted on the floor. "What's really wrong? What are you really upset about?"

"It's just...I'm just..." She came to rest from her struggles, her chest heaving in her exertions. The rope slid across her taut nipples. "I'm afraid I'll die without ever really knowing what I want. Without knowing who I am."

"Who are you then? Someone different than the girl I know? Tell me then, if you're someone else. Who are you? What are you like?"

"I don't know. That's the problem. I'm just like my father. I've been pretending to be someone else for so long, I've completely lost who I am. I've played all these roles that aren't really me for so long," she wailed, looking up at him.

"What do you mean? What kind of roles?"

"I don't know. Wayward daughter. Mean sister. Club girl. Submissive. Slut."

"You mean you aren't really a slut?"

She responded to his joke with a gaze like poison. "Untie me."

"I'm kidding, Kat."

"Let me go. I don't want to do this. I don't want to talk about this."

"I know. Believe me, I know. But we're going to talk." He held the edge of the rope hard in his fist, mid-tie, not letting her unravel the progress he'd made so far, not letting her get away. "Why do you play all those roles if it makes you unhappy?" he asked.

"I don't know."

"Think about it. To fulfill people's expectations? To hide?"

"I don't know! Untie me. Please!"

"Okay, answer me one thing first. Are you playing a role right now? Drama queen?" His voice sounded harder, angrier than he wanted it to. She looked up at him and burst into tears.

"Please untie me."

Ryan relented, starting to untie the knots with shaking fingers. "You know," he said in a harsh tone. "Kat...you know..."

"I just don't know how to love you," she cried out. "I'm scared."

"I'm scared too," he snapped. "I don't know if the love I feel for you will ever be returned. Because you overthink everything and you expect the worst in everything. And I've folded eight hundred and seventy eight cranes in the hopes that you might change, that you might get brave enough to love me anyway." He unraveled the rope from her, feeling numb and defeated. He didn't look at her face, at the tears that devastated him, the tears he didn't know how to stop. "I thought if I just loved you enough, everything would work out for us. I wish I knew the answers, Kat. I wish I knew—" He undid the last knot with a jerky movement and pulled the rope away from her.

"You wish you knew what?" she asked in a tremulous voice.

He looked at her, twisting the useless rope in his hand. "How to not lose you. How to keep you from getting away."

She reached out for him, an abrupt desperate movement and he drew her close. He felt her tears fall against his cheek and drip down onto his shoulder. "I don't want you to go away, Kat," he whispered hoarsely. "Not ever. Don't worry about love, marriage, ever after. All those words. Just please, please try to understand how I feel about you."

"I do." Her fingers stroked the hair above his ears. "I feel it in my heart. My father told me once—"

The phone rang. Ryan kissed her, squeezed her tightly and they let it ring. He felt her relax, felt her open to him. Her tears ceased and transformed to soft sighs of pleasure.

A moment later, the phone rang again.

Fortune

* * * * *

Ryan hadn't been able to make much of Elena's hysterical ramblings about Dmitri. It was part-Russian, part-English and part-gibberish. What he did understand was the gravity of the situation and the abject terror in her voice. He and Kat dressed and drove to St. Elizabeth's Hospital where the Argounovs had taken over the waiting room. He left Kat with her sobbing sisters and went with Elena to talk to Dmitri's doctor.

Kat's father had been admitted to the hospital with a splitting headache. Brain scans revealed a *glioblastoma multiforme*, a cluster of aggressive tumor cells. It wasn't an uncommon form of brain cancer but it was a serious one.

Ryan felt the doctor exaggerated Dmitri's chances of survival. He knew the prognosis was actually very grim. Ryan struggled with his own dread and sadness privately, letting Elena and her children believe, just for a while, that Dmitri had a chance. And he did have a chance at a few more months, with radiation and chemotherapy. Or surgery, if the tumor was operable.

In the waiting room, Ryan explained the medical terms and procedures to the whole family as well as he was able. Like the hospital doctor, he found himself glossing over the hard realities, obscuring the true depth of Dmitri's peril. They hung on every word, searching for hope and reassurance. Elena hugged him and sobbed against him. "Dr. Ryan, you give us so much comfort. You are very smart man, smart doctor. Brain doctor."

Ryan tensed, waiting. It was Kat who suggested it first, with her big green eyes full of tears. "You have to do the surgery, Ryan. You're the only one who can do it. I know you could save him. You're so good at what you do."

Ryan was already shaking his head but Elena grasped him with a new surge of hope.

"Yes, why do I not realize this? You can do his surgery. You are family. You must do it."

"I can't," he said gently. "I don't have privileges here."

"We can have him moved to another hospital," blurted Kat. "One of the ones where you do have privileges. I mean, this is your field, isn't it? Brain tumors and stuff?"

"Yes, it is, Kat. But it's not that simple." His gaze pleaded with her, begged her to understand. Surgery may not even be an option, and if it is, it will be a highly risky procedure. *Don't you see? I don't want to be the one who kills him. Don't make me be that person.* "Let's wait and get more information," he hedged. "They'll need to do some more tests and nail down exactly what treatment he's going to need going forward."

But the tests and hurried consultations revealed that surgery was necessary, and Ryan knew it would be best to have it done at his hospital, Boston General. Even worse, he knew he was the most qualified surgeon on staff to do it.

At home that night, Kat was racked by fears and worries. "We should have known," she sobbed against his shoulder. "His headaches. His strange moods. We should have made him go to the doctor sooner."

"No, Kat. It's not your fault. These types of tumors appear and grow rapidly. They're very aggressive—" He clamped his mouth shut but she'd already heard the truth in his voice. After all his careful efforts to preserve hope, she heard the truth of it. She stared at him.

"He's going to die, isn't he? He doesn't have a chance."

"There's always a chance, Kat," Ryan insisted through the tightness in his throat.

"No. Oh, no." She didn't believe his backpedaling. He wouldn't have believed it himself. She bolted away from him, into the other bedroom where she kept her things. He thought she would slam the door, lock him out and grieve in there, but she didn't. She returned a moment later holding out two rumpled cranes in her hands. One was the crane he'd folded from the paper placemat at the diner. The other was the one

Fortune

from her hospital room, the one he'd made from newspaper after she fell down the stairs.

"Here's two more," she said. "Show me how. Show me how to make them. I'll help you make a thousand. Please, I need your wish." She was pleading, as abject and desperate as he'd ever seen her. "I'll give it back. I'll return your wish and all that work you did, I promise, but I need it for my father. Please, Ryan!"

He looked at the worn cranes she clutched in her palm. What could he say to that?

He showed her how to fold them and in her panic she learned quickly. They weren't as accurate and precisely folded as his, but he didn't say a word. They bent over the small squares of paper until the wee hours of the morning, and with each completed figure Kat seemed to believe more strongly that the magic of the cranes would work. That the paper symbols might really have the power to bring fortune and grant a wish. *Senbazuru.* A desperate wish for a beloved father's life. Before they were done, she'd extracted his promise to do the surgery.

When they finally went to bed she slept the sleep of the dead, but he lay awake a long time looking at the strings of one thousand cranes. At the placemat and newspaper ones at the very top of the very last string. Moments crowded his memory. Kat frowning up at him from a hospital bed. Kat fidgeting across from him at the diner, choking down the fat-free cream cheese. The look in her eyes the first time he'd tied her, when she gazed up at him with a crane in her mouth. The times he'd teased her, the times he'd comforted her. Moments of submission and moments of rebellion, moments of ecstasy. He thought of her laughter, thought of her life-filled family. Finally he succumbed to the grief and helplessness strangling him, and he wept.

* * * * *

Dmitri was moved to Boston General and his surgery was scheduled for Thursday. Ryan consulted with his team of doctors, trying not to let his personal feelings for the patient cloud his professional opinions. He still did his other work and went home in the evening feeling wrung-out and fragile, only to turn around and accompany Kat to Elena's to sit and comfort her mother. Elena—bold, vibrant Elena—was struggling. Her natural ability to comfort everyone else was sorely needed now. She could not seem to comfort herself.

They all prayed. The house vibrated with endless, fervent prayers in Russian. Even the youngest children were subdued, not really understanding why the adults were so sad, but still affected by it. Ryan prayed too, in will if not in guttural Russian exhortations.

Elena prayed hardest of all. She seemed almost in a trance. The daughters questioned her, asking why she couldn't tell them Dmitri's outcome. That was her job, after all. But in this, she could not—or would not—see. She was too afraid to look, she explained on a sob. Ryan suspected she knew, but that like him, she chose not to tell. Just in case she didn't know, he guarded his gaze from her. If she looked in his eyes she would see the future written there clearly enough.

Not that he gave up completely. It was his job as a doctor to expect miracles, to continue to press forward even if success was unlikely. He couldn't operate on Dmitri as if the end was inevitable, because that would be a betrayal. But Ryan knew, even if Dmitri survived the invasive surgery, he would not be himself anymore. Even if he survived he would have to endure chemo, radiation... None of which would stave off the insidious astrocyte cells for long. Dmitri would not be giving Kat away at her wedding. Even in a best-case scenario, Dmitri would not see the leaves start to change in the fall. Ryan wanted to tell them all, warn them to say what they needed to say before Thursday, but their stolid Russian hope was too formidable. He couldn't say the words.

Even with Kat he kept the secret. He let her believe there was hope because to do otherwise would hurt her too much. Afterward he would hold her and comfort her. If she didn't blame him.

If they all blamed him he couldn't live with himself. It was hard enough to do what he did, deal in procedures and prognoses that were, more often than not, based on a tilting fulcrum of chance and luck. The fortunate survived and the unfortunate didn't. He lived with it every day. There was really no bargaining with errant human cells and he'd long ago stopped trying. But this was the first time in his career that he truly wished he could bargain something away.

But not her. He wouldn't have given her up even for this. He let her have the cranes because he had to, but in his heart they were still all for her. For her soul, her heart, her happiness. And his happiness, which he truly believed was somehow tethered to hers.

All too soon Thursday arrived. He went into the surgery determined to do his very best work. If there was a way to save Kat's father he would find it. He was prepared. He was stone. His hands didn't shake as he patted Dmitri's shoulder and murmured words he didn't even remember to a man who wasn't totally there. For a while the surgery went well and Ryan started to feel guardedly hopeful. But then things began to go not-so-well. He knew the moment he started to lose him and then his hands began to shake.

Again the sickening slide of helplessness. *But I'm trying. I'm trying my very best. Why won't this work?* Dmitri began to seize on the table. The machines shrieked and beeped their inhuman warnings, as if Ryan wouldn't know there was trouble without their prompting. He knew he was losing him. He knew.

The trauma team jumped in and Ryan was pushed to the side, to the outskirts of the drama. His role was done now. If it had been a normal surgery he would have left the room, gone back to his office and made notes. *Unsuccessful.* He would have enumerated the steps he took to excise the tumor, the advent of the seizures, the quadrant and locus of the fatal bleed. The wheres and whys. But not this time, not yet. This time he stayed and watched as if in a dream as they worked on his lover's father. He watched Dmitri code, come back and code again. He watched until the team desisted, removed their gloves and called it. And still he stayed and watched as they sewed him back up. He wanted to apologize. He wished he had said goodbye to Dmitri before they put him under. He wished he had told him how much he respected him, that he was a good man with a treasure of a family. He wondered how he could go back in the waiting room and face them all.

He had to change into clean scrubs before he went to give them the news.

* * * * *

Kat sat hunched among her sisters and her mother. The husbands minded the children, shuttling them back and forth to the bathrooms and vending machines as needed. None of them spoke. The time for prayers and panic was over. For now, it was out of their hands. Based on the location of the tumors and the insidious nature of the particular type of cells, Ryan had put the likelihood of success—survival—at fifty-fifty. Kat knew with some sixth sense that he was inflating the actual chances. But she tried not to think of that. She tried to think of a thousand cranes, good fortune, a wish.

I wish, I wish. I wish for my father to smile at me again, to call me princess just one more time.

As soon as the door opened, as soon as she saw Ryan's drawn, blank affect, her wishes disintegrated into dust. Elena's soft, choked sob was somehow worse than her sisters' howls of mourning.

"I'm so sorry," he said, spreading his hands. "I'm so sorry I couldn't... We lost him. The tumor was too..."

His voice was tight. He shuddered a little, so slightly, but Kat saw it.

"He's gone. I'm sorry. There was always a risk. The tumor was—" His hands fell at his sides, helpless. "I'm so sorry."

Her sisters fell on Elena and wept. The husbands cried silently in that stolid manner men have, still tending the children with the robotic efficiency of necessity. A searing pain crippled Kat so that she couldn't move. *Gone.* How could he be gone just like that?

Ryan still stood across the room, the deliverer of doom. The interloper. She knew she should go to him and tell him it was okay, that it wasn't his fault. That he shouldn't be sorry for trying to help them. Some impulsive realization reached her through all the pain and shock. Just as he turned to go, she flew across the room and caught his arm.

He looked down at her. There was a tension in the arm she held, a fathomless cast to his dark gaze. He cupped her face. "I'm sorry, doll. I tried." His hand dropped away and he moved again to the door. "I can't stay. I have to finish his chart."

After he left, after they completed the excruciating exercise of saying goodbye to Dmitri's body, Kat went home with her family. The house had a feeling of quiet unreality. As she walked through the rooms it felt as if she were trespassing in another family's home. And Dmitri's small TV room, with his worn recliner... No one could bear to go near it. His absence haunted them like a ghost.

Ryan's absence haunted her too. He didn't come, not even when it neared midnight. At last, Kat left to go find him. She found him sitting up on the side of his bed in darkness, in silence. She went to him, uncertain of his mood, but he turned and pulled her into a gentle, enveloping embrace.

He'd been drinking. She could smell it on him. "Are you mad at me?" she whispered.

"No. Of course not. Why would I be mad at you?" His words slurred a little. He frightened her this way because it was so unlike him to drink. She shrank away but he held her.

Kat's head hurt and her eyes ached from crying. His somber misery dragged her down even deeper into sadness, like a weight on her heart. Bleak grief was choking her, drowning her, and Ryan, her buoy, was dark in the night. "I'm sorry I asked you to..." She couldn't say it. "I—I shouldn't have. I shouldn't have asked you to—"

"You were right, Kat. It's all bullshit." His gruff, toneless voice startled her.

"What...what's bullshit?"

"All of it. Love. Hope. Wishes." He made a sibilant sound of frustration and then he laughed. "You know what it comes down to, Kat? Blood and physiology. Cells. Reality." He groped her between the legs, an awkward aggressive pressure. She pushed away from him and he stood, dumping her from his lap. His arms rose at his sides and he stood over her like a furious dark angel. "This is it, Kat. This is what we have. And this stupid shit—"

He lurched for the cranes in the corner, the mass of strings alive with wings and delicate beaks. "Cranes. Luck. Good fortune. Bullshit!" His hands tore at the paper chains, stripping the glossy creations from their anchor, pulling them down, shredding them, crushing them. He spun on her. "You believed! When it suited you, you believed. What do you think now?"

Kat shook her head, speechless. She watched his fists close on the broken cranes in his hand and something inside her felt crushed and broken too. She backed away from the man she didn't know, this man she didn't recognize, and she ran.

*****

Fortune

Kat fled down the streets of Cambridge until she ran out of breath, until her lungs ached and then she walked, blowing convulsive breaths of condensation into the cold night air. She didn't have her coat but she barely felt the weather. She welcomed the numbness. Her walk slowed to an amble. She stopped, finding herself in a familiar place.

She gazed up at the marquee of Masquerade. An effusive group of college-aged partygoers nudged past her and pushed her forward toward the ropes. One of the bouncers smiled at her. "Hey. Long time no see. You coming in?"

Kat looked down at herself, her jeans and tee, her hospital waiting room clothes. She didn't even have her purse with her. "I don't have ID," she said, holding up her hands. Her voice sounded strange and robotic.

The other bouncer shrugged. "We know who you are. Come in out of the cold."

They led Kat under the rope, comped her in. Their kindness resonated in the emptiness of her mood, made her want to cry some more. The darkness, the smoke and music crawled over her, coating her in a familiar film. How long had it been since she'd been here? Several months by now. It seemed like a lifetime. She felt out of place as she crossed to the stairs and climbed up to the balcony. She remembered the first time they'd talked there.

You're monitoring my vices?

Should I be?

She remembered falling down the stairs and looking up to find him leaning over her. That was the first time she'd noticed that intensity in his eyes, the intensity he'd just turned on her in his bedroom, ripping down cranes and raging over... What? The helplessness of life. So many wishes unanswered. Even if you knew the future, like her mother, it didn't make it any easier to cope with when it arrived.

The view from the balcony was different, so different now. Kat went to the restroom just before one but Marla wasn't there. It was some other woman Kat didn't know. Kat slunk out the door, having no money to leave a tip anyway, thinking of what may have befallen Marla. Car accident? Aneurysm? A particularly aggressive brain tumor like her father? The dance floor was crowded now, the music almost painfully loud. Kat pushed her way through the undulating throng, then looked up into the eyes of a guy she remembered, although she couldn't recall his name. She ducked her head, changing direction, avoiding his grasping fingers, only to see another guy she'd been with once upon a time. She forced her way to the stairs, climbed to the balcony and huddled in the back corner, shaking with something like fear.

Those boys. She had been so empty back then, back when she'd played around with those boys. So miserable. Not the misery of sadness she felt now, but an encompassing, smothering misery that had nearly consumed her life. She didn't want that again. She wanted Ryan. She wanted fun and trust and that closeness he forced on her that scared her and made her feel alive. She thought of crushed cranes and his empty eyes and she knew she'd ruined everything. She'd lost everything. She turned her face to the wall and let the stinging tears come.

She'd lost all the things she never even realized she had.

* * * * *

When she'd left, he'd had the urge to drink more, to really finish the self-destruction he'd started. But then his gaze had fallen on the mass of cranes. He hated those cranes for betraying him, for betraying Kat. For not living up to the magic he believed in. Even half-drunk, he realized his mistake. He realized there was only one way to save the relationship — and it wasn't folded paper.

He gathered up every crane, one thousand in all, and stuffed them into a trash bag. It felt slightly depraved, slightly murderous, but he did it anyway. He took the bag down to the dumpster and flung it in, bringing the lid down with a bang and then set out to the club district, newly sober.

He knew she had walked and he had a pretty good idea where she would end up. The bouncers greeted him with broad smiles and when he inquired after her, gestured him inside toward the balcony. He navigated the press of bodies with a sense of dread. What would he do if he found the old Kat on the dance floor, gazing up at some asshole with a come-hither glint in her eye?

But no, that wasn't what he found. Her gaze was destitute, bleak. He hung back a moment, feeling ashamed. He was the one who was supposed to comfort her in her loss and instead he'd completely lost control.

"Poor Kat," he said softly. He had no words to express how he felt, the depth of his longing for her. The intensity of his desire to save their relationship. "I'm sorry," he finally said. "I should have been there for you tonight. I know how much you loved him."

"Yes, I did love him." Her voice faltered as she reached out for him. "But I love you too."

He clasped her close, drank in the feel and smell of her.

"I love you, Ryan. I don't want to lose you too."

"You won't lose me. I'm not giving you up. No matter what. That's what I came here to tell you."

They walked out of the smoky, noisy club together, drawing in fresh deep breaths of clear air. He wrapped his coat around her and they made their way back home hand in hand, talking about deep and soulful things like love and loss, luck and misfortune, minds and hearts and connection. All the things they'd been too afraid to talk about before. When they got home it was after two in the morning and still they talked as they took each other's clothes off, as he led her to bedroom.

She didn't mention the missing cranes when her glance flitted to the empty corner and he didn't explain what he'd done with them. He made love to her without any rope, without any collar. He held her down with his hands and his body alone and slid into her, taking on all her shuddering ecstasy and grief. He soothed her and comforted her, reveling in the perfect completion of being inside her. He felt her skin against his like a promise, soft velvet proof that he held her, he had her. She was his.

"I'm yours, I'm yours," she sighed as he loved her.

"Yes, you are," he whispered back. *At last.*

Chapter Twelve
Six Months Later

ဢ

"Oh my—oh my *god*—" Kat threw her head back in the dim light of the lazy August morning. She pulled at the knotted rope that bound her hands together and tethered them to the headboard of Ryan's bed. She spooned back against him, grinding her hips as he reached around to twist her nipples vigorously. "Oh— Oh— *Please!*"

"Shh." Ryan chuckled against her ear and placed a hand over her mouth. "The windows are open."

"Mmph...don't...care..." she mumbled against his palm. "Don't care...don't care..."

"If you don't quiet down," he said in a lower voice, "I might have to punish you for it later." Her pussy clenched on his cock, his softly spoken words settling in her pelvis with a low hum. "And I don't think you'll like it."

Kat wasn't sure about that, but she was beyond caring anyway. "Oh my god," she squealed behind his hand as he used the other to reach between her legs and tease her clit in long torturous strokes. Each time he entered her from behind, he hit her spot and made her shudder and tense up at the sheer, singing pleasure. "Oh please, please, please never stop doing that."

As soon as she said it, he stopped. She let out a strangled moan. "Please, Sir. I said please!"

"If you want it, control yourself. Be quieter. I've told you what I want."

She swallowed another wail, let his words sink into her brain when most of her thought was centered between her thighs.

"Quiet...quiet..." he whispered. "And I'll make you come. Eventually," he added. "But you have to be a good little girl."

Kat clamped her mouth shut and turned her head into the pillow. If he didn't let her come soon, she would die. She would just literally expire. He'd been teasing her all morning, bringing her to the edge and denying her. "Please let me come," she whispered through clenched teeth.

"Hm. I don't know. I kind of like you all frustrated like this. I think I'll enjoy our engagement party more if I know you're stewing in your juices, edged to within an inch of your horny little life."

"You're a fucking sadist," she bit out before she could stop herself. His only answer was a self-satisfied snicker.

"Language, Ekaterina. That's no way for my future bride to behave."

"I'll do anything...please...just please let me..."

"Okay." His cool voice rose over her mindless babbling as his cock bumped closer between her legs. "Let's bargain."

Kat groaned. His "bargains" generally involved choosing between horrible choice number one and horrible choice number two. He pinched one nipple hard and leaned closer to her ear. She tried to concentrate through the sharp pain and the resulting flare in her aching center. In typical form, he presented her with two equally sadistic options.

"My sweet little doll. You can either go to the party today edged like this, or you can orgasm now and go to the party with welts on your bottom and a plug in your ass."

Kat tensed and shook her head against the pillow. "You're mean. *So* mean! Maybe I shouldn't marry you after all."

"Oh," he laughed, twisting one hand in her hair. "You're going to marry me. Now stop whining and decide."

"Well...what kind of welts?"

Ryan laughed harder. "Will that make a difference? Hmm. Cane welts. That's sure to make you fidget every time you sit down."

Kat considered, wondering for the millionth time how she could have fallen for such a sadist—and how he managed to always keep her panting after him for more. God, she hated the cane. But the idea of not coming, of having to sit through hours of celebration and family conversation with this dissatisfied ache in her pussy was more than she could bear. She took a breath and threw her head back against him, swiveling her hips, trying to wrench her own orgasm away from him without his help. But with her hands tied she couldn't touch her clit, couldn't set that final avalanche in motion. He tsked and withdrew from her, holding her hips still. "Decide, naughty girl, or I'll make the decision for you."

"I—I want to come," she said with a sigh.

He thrust back into her at once, hit her spot again with an accuracy that always amazed her.

"Does that feel good, baby?" he asked.

"Yes. Oh, yes!"

"I guess you really want to come by now. I bet you're really dying to."

She sobbed, past words, past pleading.

"I don't want to hear a sound," he whispered as his hand snaked down her hip. "Twelve strokes if you make noise when you come. Only eight if you're quiet as a mouse."

Kat held her breath as his fingers again slid between her legs, slipping moisture and unbearable sensation across her clit and fanning the stuttering spark to a fire. She ignited into a long-awaited orgasm, the throbbing pleasure licking along every nerve and muscle. She held the cry of relief inside her like a secret and let her convulsing body express to her lover the intensity of her release. He came too, his deep powerful thrusts and masculine grunts only exacerbating the euphoria she felt.

But too soon he pulled away from her, a satisfied smile on his face. "Just eight then, mousie. I see my sub can be motivated by pain."

"I can be motivated by orgasms too," Kat grumbled. "But you don't seem to care about that."

"Oh, I care." He slapped her ass lightly as he rolled off the bed and went for his implements of torture. "But sometimes I'd rather make you squirm. Down onto your tummy, Kat."

She was squirming all right. Her insides had that funny feeling they always had when she knew he was going to hurt her. A dread and yet a longing for the pain because it came at his hands. He laid the cane beside her on the bed as she settled on her stomach. She turned her head the other way.

"Spread your legs." His sharp voice had her parting her legs without a second thought. "All the way."

She spread them wider. When he caned her he always tied her hand and foot. He used rope to circle her ankles and draw each leg taut toward its respective bedpost. When he was finished, she was stretched and spread wide open. Vulnerable. Trembling. And wet. God, she was still horny. Ryan's extended edging session had left her so keyed-up that even her massive orgasm hadn't completely assuaged the ache. As he pressed a lubed anal toy to her asshole, she found herself grinding her clit against the sheets beneath her. Her breath was coming in short, panting gasps. The plug stretched her, filling her with the familiar sensation of impalement. It was a smooth stainless plug, the one he put in her for extended wear. She thought of the party, the way her family's celebrations tended to last long past early afternoon into nightfall. She buried her face in the covers and groaned.

Ryan ignored her, standing beside the bed and taking up the cane. "Ready?"

Fortune

She let out a whimper. Ryan paused, then crossed to shut the window first. He returned and Kat braced. The first cane stroke fell across her ass like fire, a different type of fire than the conflagration of orgasm. This was fire that hurt. The second stroke fell and she cried, pleading. She always broke right away, started begging and crying. She never used the safeword though. She didn't really need it. She'd learned by now to breathe through each blow, to subdue the rising panic that made the pain more difficult to bear. He laid each stroke in a precise lattice that she could feel on her ass cheeks. The cumulative effect was a cluster of stunning pain that made her ass feel swollen to twice its usual size.

"Oww! Please," she cried in desperation.

"Nearly done. Two more strokes. Be brave."

The next one was the hardest and Kat screamed, tears squeezing from her tightly shut eyes. *Just one more, just one more.* And then the agony of sitting and shifting on the welted tracks all through the engagement party. You get engaged to a sadist, you pay the price. Kat gazed up at her trapped fists, at the round, glittering diamond on her ring finger. In her heart, Kat knew it was a price she was only too eager to pay.

The last stroke made her whole body jerk, made her clench on the hard metal plug inside her. The aching fire penetrated, spread and then converted into the same dull throbbing that covered the rest of her bottom. She felt her muscles relax as he put the cane away and then returned to her. He knelt next to her on the bed and slid his hands up her parted thighs, then over the welts on her bottom. He licked and kissed each cheek, but she was too drained to react now.

"Not so horny anymore, little girl?"

"Just relieved it's over."

He chuckled softly and moved over her, straddling her back, reaching up to the rope around her wrists. Lazily he undid the knots, flipping over the ends and unraveling rope until she was untied. He leaned to push her hair away and lick the back of her neck.

"I think I might try something new today."

Oh. Wonderful, Kat thought with equal parts curiosity and dread.

He drew the rope down over her shoulders, down her back and across her hips. His fingers began to work at it again, securing it around her waist. Her legs were still parted wide and held fast, so he had no problem reaching under her hips and pulling the tails between her legs. It finally dawned on her that he was tying her into some kind of crotch harness. She moaned as he worked a knot into the tails, positioning it on her clit and pulling the rest up and over the flange of the plug lodged in her ass. He tied it off in the back.

"Wow. I really like that. What do you think, Kat?"

She moaned into her arm.

"After you shower, before you get dressed for the party, I want you to report back to me so I can tie you up like this. Can't have you forgetting who you belong to at your own engagement party."

As if, Kat thought as he started to undo the ankle ties. Rope or not, he had her tied up tight.

* * * * *

Ryan watched her circulate around the party, his face composed in an affectionate, bemused expression. He had to hand it to her, she managed to move around pretty smoothly considering the cane tracks on her ass and the rope on her clit. Not to mention the plug jammed in her backside. *Can't have you forgetting who you belong to...*

It had taken him too much time and effort to make her understand who she belonged to, to ever let her forget. Not that he was worried. Not anymore.

Fortune

Elena swept up beside him and gave him the thirtieth hug of the day. She followed his gaze to where Kat stood in her cream-colored floral dress, gossiping with her sisters. "You know," Elena said. "I knew this secret of yours. I knew it all along."

He looked over at her in alarm until he realized she wasn't referring to the secret torment he was visiting on her daughter. "Of course you knew," he said with the teasing cheek of a soon-to-be son-in-law. "Any fortune-teller worth her salt would have seen it coming a mile away."

"Oh, you." She swatted him. "You joke, but I tell you I knew. When I saw you at the hospital, when she fall down the stairs and bust her silly head. I knew then. You stood there in your fancy white coat and talk about tests and stare at her charts. I knew." Elena gave him a coquettish smile. "I knew very well."

Ryan returned a sly grin. "Okay. Maybe. But I knew too. Before Kat did, anyway."

"Oh, Dr. Ryan, you listen and I tell you. My daughter is sometimes a scatterhead."

"You mean scatterbrain?"

"Head, brain. Whatever," she said, waving her hand at him. "But you love her. This is a good thing. You see she needs something extra to be happy. She needs...how do you say it in English? A *firm hand*."

Ryan choked on the olive he'd just swallowed, prompting Elena to pound him on the back. "Um...okay. I'm fine, Mama." He said it Ma*ma*, the way the others said it. She beamed and then regarded him with a more sober expression.

"Now, you see, you are part of our family. We watch out for each other. We watch out for you. You become part of our family at the wedding, but really it is long before that. You understand?"

"Yes, I think I do understand," Ryan said, touched by her words.

"You become my family when you try so hard to save Dmitri. Dmitri told me many times what a special and good man you are. And he was right." Elena's eyes welled up a little, the way they still did whenever she talked about her late husband. But she pressed on through the mist, her voice effusive as ever. "I know you try. You know none of us ever blame you, ever be mad at you. You know this. For what you did, you stay forever in my heart."

Ryan squeezed her arm softly. He had known that all along, but to hear it out loud silenced some part of the niggling guilt that still haunted him sometimes. "You've done so much for me too," he replied in a soft voice, remembering her long-ago trip to the gift shop. Her "*Yes. And Yes.*"

"But this is enough emotional talk," said Elena. "We are here to celebrate, yes? Go on. Go and be with your bride."

Ryan was sent off with another smothering hug. He sidled up to Kat and slipped his arm around her waist, feeling for the harness. He had taken mercy on her and used his thinnest rope, almost a twine, so her secret wouldn't be detectable. The less-bulky rope had ended up suiting his purposes. He'd made a wicked large knot out of another, scratchier natural rope, and the thinner twine made it possible to pull the knot right up against her clit. She shifted as his hand moved down over her sore ass cheeks and he saw the telltale shiver that let him know the knot was doing its job.

"How are you holding up?" he asked as he drew her out of earshot of the other party guests.

"I'm...barely surviving."

"I'm happy to hear it," he said with a grin. "I know I'm having a really fun time watching you suffer."

"I think at our wedding ceremony you should have to wear weights on your balls," she snapped back.

Ryan laughed. "Careful, or I may reconsider that orgasm I'm thinking of giving you later. You're going to be pretty wrought-up by the time we get home. Aren't you, doll?"

She looked up at him, the wonderfully precious look of a tormented subby.

"I can't wait to go home with you later," she whispered.

"Aren't you enjoying your party?"

"I am... But there are other things I enjoy more."

"Lucky for me." He leaned down to kiss her, using his body as a shield to reach down and press against the knot. She moaned into his mouth. He let go, deepened the kiss and assailed her lips with all the elemental passion he felt. She went soft and loose against him, wrapping her arms around his neck as he pulled her closer.

The sound of applause and Russian catcalls caught and spread, rising in volume behind them in a bedlam of jubilant noise. Ryan raised a hand to wave an acknowledgement. Kat had been lost in the magic of the kiss, but started giggling against his lips, then pulled away as they both started laughing. She looked up at him and he drank in the sight of her laughing so hard she could barely catch her breath.

* * * * *

Back at home he unwrapped the rope from her hips and crotch, smoothing his hands over the red lines the ropework left behind. They didn't worry him. They would fade. He ran his fingers over the knot that had been pressed to her clit and the rope that had nestled between her pussy lips, looking up at her lasciviously. "Soaked. Just soaked. You'll have to clean this rope later."

"Yes Sir," she murmured with a guilty grin. He thought she would agree to anything in the mood she was in right now. But then, so would he.

On the way home Kat had showed him the wedding invitations she wanted, lightly speckled artisan paper with ornate script in English and Russian. At the top of each invitation, she planned to affix a miniature paper crane.

At first he had run cold on the idea. He told her he thought the invitations would be better without them. She had grown silent, accepting his opinion, but he knew she was disappointed. So he had asked, "Why?"

"Why?" Kat looked confused. "Because those cranes went through a lot of ups and downs with us."

"I know, Kat. But that night—"

"That night was just one night. I remember a lot of other nights looking up at those cranes in the corner of your bedroom. Thinking about…"

"Thinking about what?"

Kat considered a moment. "Possibilities."

Possibilities. They certainly had plenty of those now. He had ultimately okayed the invitations—her happy smile had been worth it. And really, all that mattered to him was getting his ring on her finger. The rest of it—the wedding, the parties, the white dress—that was for Kat and her family, and his parents. The honeymoon was for him. He felt as if he was already on it as he nudged Kat toward the bed. He pushed her onto her back, then opened her thighs and lowered his lips to kiss her wet slit as she arched beneath him. He fed on her familiar taste, enjoying her tiny shivers and shudders and the way she clutched at his hair. He stopped before she got too far along and flipped her over, pulling her hips up so he could slide into her wet pussy. He pushed her shoulders to the bed, taking his time, enjoying the delectable view and the sensations.

"Hey, doll," he said in a low voice. "Exactly who is going to fold all those little paper cranes? You have a huge family."

She looked back over her shoulder at him with an impish grin.

"Oh, hell no," Ryan chuckled. "Think again. I've already folded more than my share."

Fortune

She twisted her hips with a sigh as he fell forward and reached beneath her to stroke her breasts and tug on her nipples.

"Ohhhh..." she sighed. "I think...I think we can fold them together. Together..."

Together, Ryan thought. Kat was already tensing, nearing orgasm, the result of several hours of foreplay.

"Sir, can I come? Please may I come?"

"Wait for me, baby," he said in a gruff voice, laden with emotion. God, how he loved her. His deepest wish. His good fortune. However he earned it, it was right there clasped beneath his hands. "Let's come together, Kat," he said against her ear.

Together. He would fold a million cranes with her if she wanted it. A billion. *Yes*.

Also by Annabel Joseph

ebooks:
Deep in the Woods
Fortune

Print Books:
Deep in the Woods

About Annabel Joseph

ಜು

Annabel Joseph is a writer of erotic fetish novels that explore the drama, romance and beauty of power exchange. She especially loves to craft stories that take place in the world of the arts; her characters are often artists, dancers, writers or performers, with all the creative energy that entails. Most of all, she strives to build deep relationships between characters and deliver those moments that make readers laugh or cry.

Annabel loves to hear from her fans via her website or email, and she can also be found on Twitter. Besides writing, Annabel enjoys walking, hiking, dancing, making art, shopping at Anthropologie, playing Rock Band and wearing vampy lipstick.

ಜು

The author welcomes comments from readers. You can find her website and email address on her author bio page at www.ellorascave.com.

Tell Us What You Think

We appreciate hearing reader opinions about our books. You can email us at Service@ellorascave.com (when contacting Customer Service, be sure to state the book title and author).

Why an electronic book?

We live in the Information Age—an exciting time in the history of human civilization, in which technology rules supreme and continues to progress in leaps and bounds every minute of every day. For a multitude of reasons, more and more avid literary fans are opting to purchase e-books instead of paper books. The question from those not yet initiated into the world of electronic reading is simply: *Why?*

1. *Price.* An electronic title at Ellora's Cave Publishing runs anywhere from 40% to 75% less than the cover price of the exact same title in paperback format. Why? Basic mathematics and cost. It is less expensive to publish an e-book (no paper and printing, no warehousing and shipping) than it is to publish a paperback, so the savings are passed along to the consumer.

2. *Space.* Running out of room in your house for your books? That is one worry you will never have with electronic books. For a low one-time cost, you can purchase a handheld device specifically designed for e-reading. Many e-readers have large, convenient screens for viewing. Better yet, hundreds of titles can be stored within your new library—on a single microchip. There are a variety of e-readers from different manufacturers. You can also read e-books on your PC or laptop computer. (Please note that Ellora's Cave does not endorse any specific brands.

You can check our website at www.ellorascave.com for information we make available to new consumers.)

3. *Mobility.* Because your new e-library consists of only a microchip within a small, easily transportable e-reader, your entire cache of books can be taken with you wherever you go.

4. *Personal Viewing Preferences.* Are the words you are currently reading too small? Too large? Too... ANNOYING? Paperback books cannot be modified according to personal preferences, but e-books can.

5. *Instant Gratification.* Is it the middle of the night and all the bookstores near you are closed? Are you tired of waiting days, sometimes weeks, for bookstores to ship the novels you bought? Ellora's Cave Publishing sells instantaneous downloads twenty-four hours a day, seven days a week, every day of the year. Our webstore is never closed. Our e-book delivery system is 100% automated, meaning your order is filled as soon as you pay for it.

Those are a few of the top reasons why electronic books are replacing paperbacks for many avid readers.

As always, Ellora's Cave welcomes your questions and comments. We invite you to email us at Service@ellorascave.com or write to us directly at Ellora's Cave Publishing Inc., 1056 Home Avenue, Akron, OH 44310-3502.

MAKE EACH DAY MORE *EXCITING* WITH OUR

ELLORA'S CAVEMEN
CALENDAR

☥ WWW.EllorasCave.com ☥

Discover for yourself why readers can't get enough of the multiple award-winning publisher Ellora's Cave. Be sure to visit EC on the web at www.ellorascave.com to find erotic reading experiences that will leave you breathless. You can also find our books at all the major e-tailers (Barnes & Noble, Amazon Kindle, Sony, Kobo, Google, Apple iBookstore, All Romance eBooks, and others).

www.ellorascave.com

CPSIA information can be obtained at www.ICGtesting.com
Printed in the USA
LVOW08s1122290614

392202LV00001B/145/P